Archibald Birt

Castle Czvargas

A Romance being a Plain Story of the Romantic Adventures of two Brothers

Archibald Birt

Castle Czvargas
A Romance being a Plain Story of the Romantic Adventures of two Brothers

ISBN/EAN: 9783744735483

Printed in Europe, USA, Canada, Australia, Japan

Cover: Foto ©Andreas Hilbeck / pixelio.de

More available books at **www.hansebooks.com**

CASTLE CZVARGAS

A ROMANCE

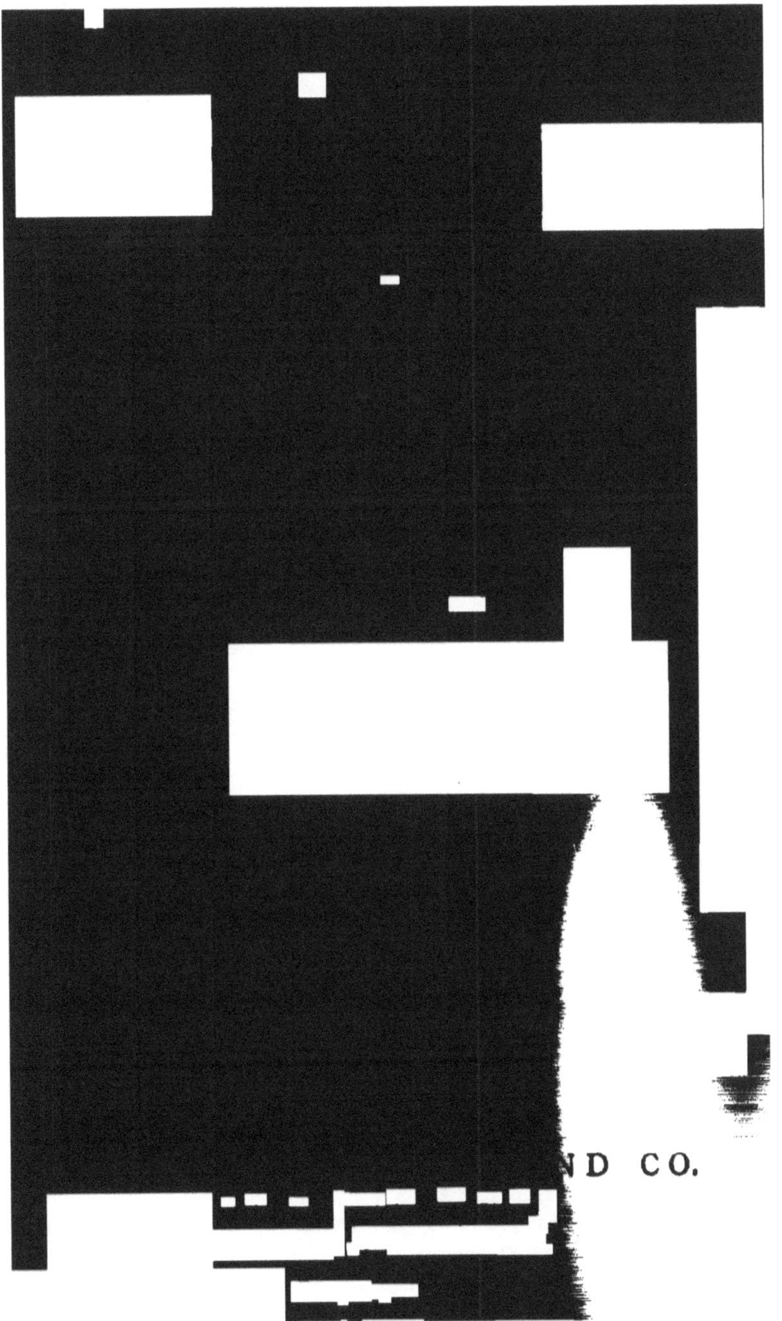
ND CO.

TO

MY FATHER

AND THE MEMORY OF

MY MOTHER

CONTENTS.

CONTENTS.

PAGE

CASTLE CZVARGAS.

CHAPTER I.

HOW DAUBENEY AND I PLAYED AT THE TAUNTON
FAIR; AND OF DAUBENEY'S GOING AWAY.

IT was not until the month of August in the year 1666, that our mother allowed Daubeney and me to enter into the public games which were played at the Taunton Fair, though my brother and I had viewed them each year since, after the joyful return of King Charles II., the Fair had been held. Now we had for some time past (at least I had, though Daubeney showed not the same eagerness) desired much to try our strength and skill against the youths of the County, and but for our love for our mother, would have done so. But about a week before the Great Fair of 1666 (when the championship matches of the County would be played), it so happened that

A

Mistress Frodsham of Tolland rode over in her coach to visit our mother at Wiveliscombe, and spoke with much pride of her son John, who had won the Belt for wrestling for the past two years, and was like to do so again, mocking at our mother for her fears concerning us, and saying that we had better have been born girls, so that she might the more easily have kept us out of the danger of getting hurt. And our mother was angry, for that she was proud of her sons (as mothers ever are). At this moment, as chance would have it, Bess came into the room, bearing a cup of Tea to Mistress Frodsham (this being a new kind of drink but recently brought from China, and much esteemed by the ladies of quality), and seeing a flush on her mother's face, asked what ailed her; and she, still angry, told Bess to bring Daubeney and me to her.

When we came in, hot from our sword play, and had made our bow to Mistress Frodsham, our mother asked if we would like to wrestle at the Taunton Fair.

"Yes, indeed would we!" I cried; for Daubeney was ever slower of speech than I, though he was fifteen months older.

" Are you not afraid of the danger of being hurt?" said our mother. And I only laughed, seeing a twinkle in her eyes ; and I looked at Daubeney, who was smiling softly. Then our mother smiled proudly back to us, as we stood before her, and from us her eyes went to the look of amusement on the large red face of Mistress Frodsham, and she turned quickly back to us and said :—

" Go tell your father that I wish you both to play at the Taunton Fair, and ask him if you may."

And we went out, wondering and delighted at this chance, and I ran and told our father. He, looking up from the book he was reading, as though he had not heard me, said :—

" Yes, Frank, if your mother wishes it, of course." And thereupon, without, I am sure, any knowledge of what I had asked or he had granted, he returned again to his book. But I ran out, and calling to Daubeney, bade him saddle his horse, as I did mine, and in a few minutes we were cantering gaily on the road to Taunton. For I was fearful that our mother would repent that she had let us, and I wished to have our names upon the lists, so that, having this to hold up to her, she might be ashamed to have us draw back.

Daubeney and I easily reached the Taunton market-place before sunset, and wrote our names upon the paper which was nailed up within the doorway of the booth that was being builded for the Fair. When this was done, I was filled with a great sense of delight, and I read aloud what we had written down : ' " Daubeney Nutcombe, of Wiveliscombe, age 21, height 6 feet 3 inches, weight 235 lbs. Francis Nutcombe, of Wiveliscombe, age 20, height 5 feet 10½ inches " (I was very careful of that same half-inch), " weight 190 lbs."

Then we repaired to the " King Charles II." Inn (for every village and town had now a King Charles II. Inn, where a few years before there were none), and ate some bread and cheese, and having nothing further to do, we jogged quietly back on our twelve-mile ride to Wiveliscombe ; at least Daubeney was quiet, though I chattered eagerly of our chances, and of the hope of winning the Wrestling Belt. For, in truth, there was nothing in which I delighted more than in a bout of wrestling, though there were few exercises that took me out of doors and away from my books in which I did not take great pleasure. But with Daubeney it was different, for, for all his size and strength, he was ever of a more studious turn, resembling in this matter the disposition of our father.

It was dark, except for the light of the stars, when we neared the gates leading to our house, and as we entered them, we met a stranger riding out. We stared at him, and he at us, but except to say "Good-night," none of us spoke, only that I remarked as Daubeney and I rode on that it was strange to meet one whom we did not know, coming from our own house. But when we went into the house we became aware of some sort of trouble in the manner of our father and mother. She, who was a very beautiful and cheerful lady, with the fairest possible hair and the bluest eyes, and so clear a pink colour to her cheeks that many of the younger beauties of our parts envied her her complexion, looked as though she had been weeping. And Bess told us that, in truth, she had; for that a messenger had ridden from Plymouth (who was doubtless the stranger that Daubeney and

I had met) with a packet from our uncle Frederick, containing the news of the death, at Munich, of our uncle John, our mother's brother.

So that our supper, which I had thought to make lively with talk of the approaching Fair, was taken in a sad silence.

During the next week, Daubeney and I did constantly practise in wrestling, and in the use of the sword; and though he was better than I in the sword-play, yet I held my own with him in wrestling, and was more often the conqueror. For though my brother's bodily strength was greater than mine and he had much advantage from his height and weight, I was the more active and firmer on my feet. Moreover, I was possessed of enormous strength in my arms, and so large was the muscle of the upper part of my arm, that when I doubled up my elbow the muscle did not harden, as is its manner with all whom I have questioned on this matter.[1] I do not tell you this in boast, but only that you may know what manner of men my brother and

[1] The most powerful man of my acquaintance has just such a biceps muscle as that described.—[ED.]

I were, for the better understanding of my story. For I am only as God made me, and take no undue pride, but a great thankfulness in my strength.

That there was something in the tidings which the messenger from Plymouth had brought, beyond the news of her brother's death, that our mother was not wishful to reveal to us, I was certain; for, during the time before the day of the Fair, she was particularly fond, and more especially did she show her love for Daubeney, following him, wherever he went, with her eyes which were too often filled with tears. And our father, too, was more quiet even than was his wont, pacing to and fro on the garden walks with his hands clasped behind him and his head bent down, for many hours of the day, to the neglect of his favourite studies.

When, however, the great day for which we had been looking, came, Daubeney and I, with no trouble on our minds, and no suspicion of what was coming to us, rode away briskly in the early morning. Bess would have come with us, but her tender age (she was but fifteen), and the fear that

she might be hustled by the crowd while
Daubeney and I were at our matches, and
so unable to protect her, kept our mother
from letting her go.

When we reached the playing-booth, we
found that there were but seventeen entered
for the wrestling, many who had given their
names at the first, withdrawing for fear of
John Frodsham. He was indeed a great
man, being within an inch of Daubeney in
height, and weightier; but I had no fear of
him either on my brother's account or my
own, for though he had great strength, he
possessed but little wit, which I think of
greater importance in a wrestling match.

The first matches were without interest,
except those in which a young fellow called
Markleigh, of Bridgewater, was engaged; for
he weighed but 155 lbs. and was slight in
figure, but most nimble with his feet, and
threw many youths who were stronger and
weightier than himself. At the last Markleigh, Frodsham, Daubeney and I were left,
and when we drew the lots it fell that
Daubeney should face Frodsham, and
Markleigh me.

In my first bout with Markleigh, I was taken by surprise, regarding him, in error, as of no great strength or skill ; for he sprang towards me suddenly, gripping me with the under-catch below my arm-pits, and tripping me cleverly with his leg behind mine he threw me to the ground before I had time to keep my feet. And I got up, shamed that, after all my hopes, I should be thrown so simply by so small a man.

Then Daubeney and Frodsham faced each other, and my brother, after a short struggle, threw the other heavily with a neat cross-buttock, turning before ever Frodsham could stay him, the two crashing to the ground with Daubeney uppermost ; and the huge weight of Frodsham with Daubeney's upon him, brought them down with so much force that Frodsham would not face my brother again, saying that he had strained his wrist in the fall ; though, in truth, as I believe, he liked not the thought of being beaten by one of us Nutcombes.

In my second bout with Markleigh I was more wary, and with a sudden spring gripped him round the body close above the hips, and before he could stay me, I cast him lightly over my shoulder. So that now, each of us two having won a bout, the chance of facing Daubeney and wrestling for the Belt would fall to the conqueror in the third. I had well-nigh lost my chance in my eagerness, for Markleigh, seeing how that he could not hope to throw me except by a sudden under-catch and a trip with his nimble feet, dodged round and round me for some minutes, refusing to engage till, angered by the waste of time, I threw up my arms and let him take me as he would. But I was ready for him, leaning forward so that he could not trip me with the back-heel or get me from my feet, and grasping his chest over his arms I gripped and gripped him till I feared his ribs would crack; he twined his nimble legs about mine, trying with all his strength to trip me; but I stood firm, ever tightening my hold of him, till at length, his breath leaving his chest, his arms fell loose to his sides, and he lay wriggling helplessly in my arms, so that I gently put him on the grass. But when he rose, and we shook each other by the hand, I was well pleased to see how the crowd cheered him for his pluck.

Now there remained but Daubeney and me, and after a short rest I stood and faced him, and a great cheer arose as we grasped hands, smiling, for we were well known, our father being a man of some importance in the County of Somerset.

I had only one fear of Daubeney, that he should get the under-catch ; for all his tricks I knew, having wrestled every day with him since I could walk.   But if he got the under-catch he would always " break my back " (as we called it) by casting all his weight upon me and bending me back and back, without the need to use his feet for tripping, until I could no longer withstand against him ; for he knew my little trick of feinting to fall, and as he loosened his hold to spring up suddenly again ; he knew this so well, that it was of no avail to me.

And so it happened in our first bout, my foot catching in a tussock of grass as we fought for the grip, I stumbled, and Daubeney's arms shot under mine, holding me tight.   Slowly, surely, towering above me, and smiling in my face, he pressed me back and back, until I lay flat upon the grass under him.   But in the second bout I threw him quickly with my most favourite trick of a feint of casting my body to one side, and as he balanced himself, straining against this side, I flung all my weight suddenly upon the other, and he fell fair. And a great cry greeted this fall, for the people always like to see the smaller man win, and they could not but be pleased by the friendly spirit shown by us, brothers.

The third and conquering bout was long and hard. We gripped equally, and I clung to this with all my strength, knowing that if I lost it for a moment and let his arms get under mine, I should be beaten. For a long time we swayed to and fro, backwards and forwards, the muscles of our bodies strained to their utmost, our legs planted firmly, in that we each feared to use them in tripping lest the other should be prepared and so gain an advantage, our breath coming, too, in great noisy gasps: and all watched us silently, wondering who should win. But at the last I did, throwing all my weight suddenly against him as he recovered from a stumble, and with my foot behind his heel, as Markleigh threw me, so now I threw Daubeney on his back.

And so I won the Belt, and I was very pleased to get it, as was Daubeney that I did. He and I met again in the contest with swords, but in this sport he easily defeated me and all others that he met, and so he, too, won a Belt. And after that the prizes had been handed to us, and the crowd had cheered, and we had slaked our thirst with great draughts of cider, we rode away, happy in our success, and little thinking that the next time we should wrestle would be in the Castle of Czvargas, of whose existence we had then no slightest breath of knowledge.

Bess came running out to meet us as we cantered up the drive, and when we told her of our success, hastened off, skipping and waving her hands, to give the news to our mother. But I called her back and questioned her as to what she had thought to tell our mother.

"That Dubs and you have won the Belts," she said.

"Never mind about the Belts," I answered, "but tell her that Dubs threw Master John Frodsham so heavily that he was afraid to face him twice for fear of the danger of being hurt!" And I laughed. For women are strange creatures, prizing greatly the honours that men gain, and thinking little of the joy of fighting, but much of the glory of winning, and more than all, of the delight of having sons stronger and skilfuller than those of other women. Yet, when Mistress Frodsham came again, which she did within the week to learn the news, our mother said no word to her of the wrestling, only in her eyes there was a look of pride and triumph which the other lady could not fail to see.

We were very merry over our supper, but as soon as it was done, my father rose, and placing his hand on Daubeney's shoulder, said gravely: "Daubeney, my son, I wish to speak with you in private; come with me." And Daubeney rose from his seat at the table, and walked out with him. Then, without a word, but with a firm tightening of the lips, our mother slowly followed them, leaving Bess and me to wonder what it might mean. For though I questioned her, Bess could tell me nothing except that our mother had wept much while we had been away in Taunton. So we waited for Daubeney's return, sitting before the fireplace in the dining-hall; and in the space of an hour he came and told us. His face was more grave even than ordinary, but I saw that his cheeks were flushed, and that his eyes had an eager look in them.

" I am going to Munich," he said, answering our noisy questions, as he took his seat between us.

"To Munich!" Bess and I cried in a breath, regarding him with astonishment. "To Munich? What for?"

" Yes," answered our brother, smiling at our open-mouthed surprise, "to Munich. And the reason of my going is that some one must be sent there to sign certain papers for our mother, and to receive moneys which have come to her from the death of our uncle John."

" But when must you go?" I cried, and at my question I thought that for a moment there came a look of pain into my brother's face, as as he replied :—

" On Thursday " (to-day was Tuesday); " I must start so soon in order to reach Plymouth in time to go in our uncle's ship to Venice, the same by which the news came telling of our uncle John's death."

And at that Bess and I sank back in our chairs and gazed at Daubeney. For this news was a great wonder to us, none of us ever having been farther away from home than Bristol, and then only for a few days, and with our father or mother. And now Daubeney was going to Venice and to Munich! And I understood now the reason of our mother's fond watching of Daubeney during the past week, when, for fear that our pleasure in the thought of playing at the Taunton Fair should be spoiled, she had said nothing to us of this parting.

But Bess soon found her tongue again, as did I 'for that matter, and we besieged Daubeney with questions, none of which, however, was he able to answer beyond what he had already told us, except that Bellew was going with him. Bellew was one of our serving-men, near upon forty years of age, but hale and strong, and having been with our family since he was a boy.

As we talked thus, our mother came in, and Daubeney, rising from his chair, led her to it and made her sit down, while he sprawled his great body on the floor at her feet, resting his fair head upon her lap. But she said nothing, only gently smoothing his hair with her hands and looking wistfully before her. So that, presently, Bess and I rose and stole on tiptoe from the room, leaving our mother and her eldest son together. And I was sound asleep when Daubeney came up to bed, which must have been long after, for I had tried hard to keep awake for his coming.

The next day was miserable enough ; we were all sad at the thought of Daubeney's going, and despite our efforts to appear cheerful for our mother's sake, we had all the look of mourners. But, fortunately, there was much to do in preparation for Daubeney's journey, and Bellew's, and little time in which to do it. That I envied them as I busied myself in the polishing of their pistols and swords, I need not say.

That night we all went early to bed, for the travellers had to be up betimes ; but my brother and I talked far into the night.

Of their going I shall not tell much, save that I rode out a few miles with them and my father, who was going as far as Plymouth (where Daubeney and Bellew would embark for Venice) to get and sign such papers as it was needful that my brother should have with him. As we pulled up our horses at the place where we must part, I drew off my Belt, the same that I had won in Taunton but two days before, which bore upon a silver shield the inscription: "County of Somerset. Wrestling Champion, 1666" (beneath was a space for my name, which I had not had the time to get cut), and handing it to my brother, in no very firm a voice told him to wear it till we met again. And he, smiling sadly, for he was loath to part with me that had never been parted from him before, took the Belt from me without a word, and gave me his own in its place, which he had won for sword-play. And so it came about that Daubeney wore my Belt, and I his, until we met again.

And then, with a strong grip of each other's hands, we parted; my father, Daubeney and Bellew cantering away upon the road to Tiverton, and I slowly back to Wiveliscombe and the weeping women.

CHAPTER II.

"AUF WIEDERSEHEN."

Now, after my father's return from seeing Daubeney off from Plymouth, he must needs try to persuade me to continue my studies with him; and, thinking only of how to pass the time before Daubeney should come back, I would sit with my father of a morning, trying to cudgel my stupid brains into the understanding of some Latin author. But often enough, to my great relief, my mother would come into us, and plead that I be let out to play; and my father, who I believe never refused her anything in his life, would smile and say :—

" If your mother thinks it best, Frank, it must be so. Go out and play until she shall allow me to have you back again."

And before his words were done, I would have flung down my books and hastened out to swim or to shoot; for I am only content when my inclination is suited to my task, and this is out of doors. And my mother would gather up my untidy books, and put them carefully away, and would then sit down with her embroidery beside my father, while he went on with his dry studies.

But during that time which followed upon Daubeney's going away, I was at some loss to know how to spend my play-time, now that I had no companion. So that it came about that I occupied myself much in swimming, in which, for all the coldness of the water, I practised myself daily, so that I was soon able to swim great distances without fatigue, only coming to shore to dress when the cold nipped me too severely. Of what great use this was to me afterwards, you shall presently hear.

I have not said—for, in truth, I am little used to writing, and easily forget many things which are of importance for you to understand —that Daubeney and I, and Bess also, had learnt to speak in the German tongue well and easily from our mother, who was born in her father's house in Munich, and had come to Plymouth in one of her brother's ships when

she was nineteen years old, knowing something of the English language, and desiring to
see those parts of our country at which the
ship called with merchandise. But, while at
Plymouth, our father had met her at a friend's
house, and by him she was persuaded not to
return to Munich, but to come as his wife to
Wiveliscombe; which she did, and remained
there ever since. So that she spoke in German as a native, but English at first only with
difficulty and hesitation; and even at this time
of which I am writing, her speech had a
strange purring sound, which to us, her
children, was very sweet.

In all the weary time that followed my
mother uttered no complaint, only that her
face grew paler, and the great shadows under
her eyes went deeper, and her smile more sad.
Of Daubeney we seldom spoke, fearing to
hurt her; but Bess and I would talk in
whispers by the fireside in the long autumn
evenings, wondering what our brother might
be doing, and how long before he would
return to us. Our father journeyed once to
Plymouth to get tidings of the ship, but by
bad luck this had not yet returned, nor any

other of our uncle's ships, so that we could not even know if Daubeney had got so far as Venice safely.

When six long anxious months had passed, and still no news of him, and every day showed us our mother looking more frail and our own faces more anxious, my father called me one morning to his room and spoke to me openly of his doubts and fears.

" I cannot speak to your mother, Frank," he said, "but first I wish to ask you what you think had best be done to learn some certain news of Daubeney, for that some evil has befallen him I greatly fear."

And I was pleased that my father should have thought to ask my advice on the matter, and I blurted out :—

" Let me go and look for him !"

But he, startled by my sudden words, said nothing, only looked long at me, and then fell into a deep, silent thoughtfulness. And my mind burning with the suddenness of my longing to go, I rose and gently left him to his thoughts.

But of this nothing was said that day, nor the next, nor for many days after, only that I knew my father had spoken to my mother of my words, for that she was more tender to me than before, and watched me as I had seen her follow Daubeney with her eyes before he went away. And in the end it was decided that I should go, my father telling me so one bitter evening of February, as he and I sat before the fire in his study, saying that he had learnt that one of our uncle's ships was expected to be going from Plymouth within the space of two or three weeks. And then, strangely enough, a great longing came upon me to stay at home, and I began the preparations for my journey with a sad heart. For, in truth, I was ever haunted by the hungry look in my sweet mother's eyes, and by the tears of Bess, who during the week before I went did little else but weep; and my father, too, seemed to be growing old before my very eyes.

Never can I forget, nor would I wish to, the face of my dear mother as she bade me "Good-bye." Placing her hands upon my shoulders and looking bravely into my eyes, which were filled with a great mistiness, her own brimming with tears, she steadied her voice and said :—

" Frank, my son, find Daubeney my eldest born, find him, Frank! But if you cannot," and here there came a great catch in her voice that well-nigh unmanned me, "come you back yourself: I cannot live if I lose you both . . . keep your temper, my son; hold your tongue, and be not over ready with your sword."

And at that she kissed me with a long tender embrace, and hastened away, her whole body shaking with her sobs. And I saw her but once again, for, turning to look at the old home as I rode away, I saw a kerchief waving from her window, and for a moment caught a glimpse of her face as I threw a kiss to her. Of my parting with Bess I need not speak; she, poor child, was broken-hearted at my going, and clung to me so that, at the last, I was forced to drag her almost roughly from me. My father could not leave the house to come any part of the way with me, for he had to stay and cheer my mother and sister, and God knows his task was a hard one.

I saw little of the villages and towns through which I passed on my way to Plymouth, my mind being filled with thoughts of those I had left behind, but when I reached Plymouth, the newness of everything and the excitement took much of the pain away, so that I was astonished to find how full of hope I had become. Moreover, and this was best of all, I got news from the ship of Daubeney's safe arrival in Venice after a perilous and disastrous voyage, and also that he had reached Munich, and this news I sent by messenger to Wiveliscombe, together with my last Farewells. Though this was not all I heard of Daubeney; for I learnt that he had been looked for in Venice before this, it being known that he had left Munich on his way thither, hoping to join this same ship for her voyage to Plymouth, being the one in which he had sailed before, the delay in its returning being caused by the repairs which the last stormy voyage had rendered needful.

I never again wish to feel as I did when I watched the thin line of water 'twixt the wharf and the good ship go wide and ever wider, and the shores of our beautiful country pass slowly from my sight. And, indeed, I had else to trouble me in the next week; for I was taken with so great a sickness of the sea, that I

lay groaning in my little cabin, until I feared
and even wished to die, and the tossing of the
ship upon the angry waves was like to have
killed me or ever I had travelled far. But
when I became accustomed to the movement of the ship, and was able to walk on
deck, and to watch the ever-changing beauty
of the great waste of sea, and to scent its glori-
ous smell, I thought me that a sailor's life was
very pleasant (after the first week) ; and yet
of all the sailors that I have spoken to of this
matter, some have laughed, and some have
cursed, and all have cried that they hated the
very sight of blue water, which has always
seemed a marvel to me.

I will not speak at this time of the wonders
of the city of Venice, where we arrived without accident or misadventure. Immediately
that I had left the ship, I went to the house of
one Signor Vanzetti, a merchant, to whom I
had letters from my father, and who was the
agent in this city of my uncle Frederick
Frieder. He was a shrewd little man with a
thin, yellow face, and curious black eyes, and
with small hands that he would keep always
moving before him as he spoke. From him

I heard only what I had learnt at Plymouth : that Daubeney was known to have reached my uncle's house in Munich, and to have started to return to Venice ; more than that Signor Vanzetti could not tell me. I was for starting off for Munich on the moment, but Signor Vanzetti, whose English was of the worst, and his German but indifferent, constrained me to wait, saying, as he laughed at my haste, that I could not go a-foot, and that there would be but little time that day to buy a horse, for by reason of the streets of Venice being all of water horses were something scarce, and could only be procured from some village on the mainland. But this we set about at once, going through the streets in a strange kind of barge called a Gondola. The only beast that could be bought was but a poor one, but it was the best that could be got, so I was compelled to be satisfied with it. Fretting at the delay of an hour, I was still forced to stay in Venice for the night, and to accept the hospitality of Signor Vanzetti with as good a grace as I might.

As the time for the evening meal drew near, I heard the sound of persons entering the house, whom my host went out to welcome, telling me that they were a merchant named Skoda, of Munich, and his daughter Wilhelmina, who had, two months before, come to this city on a visit, and who were going to spend the night in his house. And soon he brought them in and presented me to them.

Now, though I had been into all the houses round about our village of Wiveliscombe, and also into many others, and had met many young women who were esteemed beautiful, yet never had I eyes for any of them, being content with the sight of my mother and of Bess. But when I saw Wilhelmina Skoda, a strange shyness came over me such as I had never known before (and at which Daubeney and Bess would have laughed), and an awkwardness, so that I stammered and blushed when I tried to speak with her, so filled with wonder was I for the girl's great beauty. And when she spoke to me in English, smiling, I had nearly cried out in my surprise, for her voice was so pleasantly sweet, and the strange purring of her tongue so like my own mother's, that a great wave of home-sickness rushed over me, and I blushed

like a girl as I felt my eyes go full with tears.
And so much did this influence me, that for
many days afterwards, when my thoughts took
me back to the old home in Wiveliscombe, I
could fancy Wilhelmina Skoda there, talking
with my mother, the two purring to each
other; and Bess and she linking arms (as
is the fashion of girls), and walking together
up and down the garden.

Signor Vanzetti arranged our sitting at the
table so that he and Herr Skoda were somewhat apart from us two younger people; and
the two merchants paid no heed to us as they
talked (in Italian) about their business.

And Fraülein Skoda, smiling at my boorish-
ness, which she doubtless thought natural in
an Englishman, chattered on while we were
taking our meal, so that, listening to her light
talk, I had not much need to speak. But
afterwards, when she and I sat together before
the fire, our host and Herr Skoda being still
intent upon their talk of business, something
of the wonder and admiration of my regard,
I think, came to her; for she became more
silent, asking me questions of my home and
of England; so that I must needs speak in

my turn while she listened.   But when I told
her of Wiveliscombe, she looked up at me
with great earnestness, and said :—

"May I learn your name? for Signor
Vanzetti was something neglectful when he
presented you." (Indeed he had merely
spoken of me as "my young English friend.")

"My name," I said, "is Francis Nutcombe."   At that there came, as I thought,
an eager light into her eyes, and she raised
one hand as though she would have touched
my arm ; but she did not touch it, and I found
myself wishing that she had.

"Do they call you Master Frank?" she
said.

"Yes," I answered, and smiled at her
pleasant speaking of my name.

"Have you a brother, Daubeney Nutcombe?" she asked.

"Yes, indeed!" I cried, excited now ; "did
you see him in Munich, my brother?"

"Yes," she answered, smiling at my eagerness, "and he told me much of you—and of
your prowess," she added with a sly glance at
me.   And once more I chid myself for my
girlishness in that at the thought of Daubeney

my eyes should fill, so that I had to look away from her lest she should see.

"He is my brother, in truth," I said presently, "and never was there a braver, nor a better, nor a kinder ——" But she stopped me with her hand upon my arm.

"But he said much the same of you!" she cried. And then her merry laugh rang out in a bright peal, so that the two merchants looked up from their talk and smiled with her. And, indeed, when she laughed it was always so, that all who heard her wished to laugh too.

So we talked of Daubeney, I nothing loath, until I was ashamed of my praise of him, my brother. But she only smiled at me, and led me on to talk of Bess and of my mother and father. And when I had said all I had to say, she rose, and taking me by the hand, bade me "Good-night," saying—

"I would wish, Master Frank, that I might know them, your mother and your sister Bess, if all that you and your brother say of them be true!" And I blushed again with the shame of thinking that I had praised my own people too much, but in a moment, with a smile so winning that I looked at her with longing, she had gone; and at her going, I felt that the room was, of a sudden, strangely empty.

But I remembered that I must go early to bed, since I had to be up at daybreak for my journey on the road to Munich; and as I spoke to Signor Vanzetti, thanking him for his hospitality, Herr Skoda asked me if I would not wait until the day of his going, for that he and his daughter were also bound for Munich, and waited only until a guard of soldiers could be hired for the protection of his party on the way thither. For a moment, to my shame I say it, I hesitated, the girl's blue eyes seeming to beckon me, and causing so great a longing in me to see them once again, that I had almost yielded. But I thought of the last words of my mother, and of Daubeney, to whom an hour or a minute might mean so much, and thanking Herr Skoda somewhat roughly for his courtesy, I bade the two men " Good-night."

And I found myself wondering, as I lay down upon my bed, how much Daubeney and Fraülein Skoda had seen of each other, and how it could be that Daubeney had seen her and not loved her as I already did. But I drove the thought from me, and presently fell asleep.

I was up full early the next morning, and in the chill dawn, by candlelight, I ate my breakfast. As I finished it, Signor Vanzetti entered the room, followed by Herr Skoda and his daughter, she looking as beautiful and fresher than the evening before, the morning air bringing a colour to her cheeks and a gleam to her bluest eyes that were very pleasant to see. My host, whom I had not looked to see so early, was pleased at my surprise, and said that they had come to drink a cup of wine to my safe journey and success in the object of it. At which he poured out for each of us a glass. And I, looking at Fraülein Skoda who was standing close to me, before I drank, cried, " Auf Wiedersehen !" astonished at my own boldness ; and I saw that the colour rushed to her face as she touched the wine-cup with her lips, while I, in my clumsiness, nearly spilled my glass.

So that, after I had shaken them each by the hand, and had entered the Gondola which was to take me to the place where my horse

was waiting for me ; and after I had mounted
him and ridden forth upon my long journey,
were my eyes open or shut, I saw before me
Wilhelmina's fair waving golden hair, and her
glancing blue eyes; ay, and I could feel the
touch of her little slender hand, and hear the
purring of her voice.   And yet when next I
saw her!—but that I must tell, and many
more things in their turn, or else, writing of
her, my pen would run on until the ink went
dry.

CHAPTER III.

I HEAR DISQUIETING NEWS OF DAUBENEY, AND ASTONISH MY UNCLE.

I TRAVELLED as fast as my horses would let me, for I early changed the wretched Venice animal for a better steed, and that again for another, and arrived in Munich late in the afternoon of a day in April.

To say that my uncle Frederick was pleased to see me would be to say little. He welcomed me with open arms, and many exclamations of delight and of wonder at my coming, and also at my likeness to my mother. But in this I think that his desire to see a likeness caused him to fancy more than there was. For I am black-haired, like my father and Bess, and my eyes, so my sister has often told me, are the one brown and the other of a hazel colour. Yet, I do not know, for though I should find it difficult to tell you why, and though it would take long to find two persons more unlike, my uncle brought something of my mother to my mind, his carriage I think, and the way he held his head. He was a short and stoutly built man with an odd, wrinkled face, and a way of screwing up his eyes when he looked closely at anything that almost hid them ; his fair, soft beard reached half-way down his chest, and he was clothed in plain black clothes. When he spoke he let his words fall slowly and carefully as though he weighed each one.

As soon as I was able to speak for answering of his questions about my mother, and the reason of my coming, I entreated him to tell me of my brother Daubeney. At that his face became of a sudden very grave, and drawing his hand many times through his long beard, which was his constant habit when in thought, he took me by the arm and led me to a room opening from the hall. Here we sat down, and after a short silence, screwing up his eyes and bending towards me, he said :—

"Your brother is a prisoner of Count Czvargas in his Castle of Czvargas which —— " But I interrupted him hotly.

"A prisoner!" I cried, "Count Czvargas!

and who in the devil's name is he?" and I rose from my seat in my anger and astonishment; for to me, in truth, it was a monstrous thing that my brother Daubeney should be a prisoner to any one.

"Cht! cht! Nephew," said my uncle, "nought can be gained by calling on the devil's name; thank God, rather, that your brother is still alive!"

And I sat down, humbled and abashed by his quiet reproof, but with a strange rage in my heart at this Count Czvargas; and yet with a wild hope at the knowledge that my brother was not dead, I waited for my uncle to speak.

"Who is Count Czvargas?" he said slowly, "that would be hard to tell. But it is common talk that he is cruel and rapacious, and that he lives with a band of hired ruffians in a castle that is so strongly built that one man might defend it from the assault of an army."

"But Daubeney," I cried, "how came it that he fell into the power of this man?"

"I will tell you all I know," replied my uncle, "and I had best begin at the time that your brother left Munich. The business about which he came was somewhat longer in finishing than I had thought, and when it was done, he chose to return by way of Gralzburg and Spätz; and when I spoke to him of the dangers of this road, he laughed at me, saying that no one had molested him on his way hither, and that all things looked peaceful and orderly in the country through which he had passed. Seeing that he was determined upon going by this way, I said no more, only telling him to be careful where he rested for the night, and to conceal his money carefully about his person. I trusted to his great size and strength, and to his quiet, studious habit to keep any from molesting him. Of the Count Czvargas I did not think at all, knowing less of him then than I do now, and believing that the way by which Daubeney would travel did not lie within that part of the country in which the Count carried on his evil practices. Your brother left my house, then, with his man Bellew, on the morning of the tenth day of November, and I heard no tidings of him until the middle of the month of January, and then news came to me in a disquieting manner. On the morning of that day, there came to my house a young Bavarian peasant of the better class, asking to see Herr Friedrich Frieder. I had him brought to this room, and asked him his business. But he closed the door carefully behind him with so great an air of mystery that I was something alarmed (for, though scarce eighteen years of age, he was a great powerful fellow), and I stepped back ; he thereupon grinned foolishly, and asked me in a whisper (and all he said afterward was in the same tone, as though he feared to be heard by any other than myself, so that I spoke softly also) if I knew anything of one Daubeney Nutcombe. I started at his question, though I could not refrain from smiling at the strange manner in which he mouthed your brother's name.

" ' Yes, indeed,' I answered, ' what of him ? '

" ' I have news of him,' he said.

" ' Well, tell it me then,' I cried, ' and I pray it may be good.'

" ' No, sir !' he said, ' it is not good, but even of the worst.'

" And my heart sank at the thought of your mother's grief, for she ever spoke of Daubeney in her letters, as indeed of you and your sister, in words of great love " (so that I felt a warm rush of affection for my uncle), " and I blamed myself bitterly for that I had not kept Daubeney from returning by this way, and I cried to the man to tell me all he knew."

" ' The man who was with Herr Nutcombe is dead,' he said (and I was grieved to hear this, for Bellew had been a faithful servant and was much liked by all of us, and had taught my brother and me to ride), ' and he himself is taken a prisoner to the Castle of Czvargas.'

" At the sound of this name," my uncle went on, " I rose and paced the room in wonder and fear, but some hope, for that I had heard that the Count Czvargas was ready to release prisoners taken by him on payment of a heavy ransom.

" ' Count Czvargas ! ' I cried to the peasant, ' how came you by this news? Tell me more, man ! ' and as he hesitated, I said, ' you need not fear, you shall be rewarded.' And I sat down again and listened patiently to his story.

" ' Three weeks ago,' he said, ' I returned

to my mother's house from Gralzburg ; I was on foot, and went secretly for fear of this same Count Czvargas, who, by reason of my size, desires me for one of his guard, but which I like not, being wishful of a more honest life. While I was sitting with my mother over a cup of wine, she showed me some papers which she had found upon the person of a dead man lying on the roadside near to her house. She told me that this man had slept the night before in our house, and that he seemed to be the servant of another who was with him, and who was of great size.'

" 'And did you read the papers?' I asked him.

" 'No, sir ; I cannot read,' he answered, grinning at my question, 'but when I returned to my work at Gralzburg, I showed them to the priest, and he spoke to my master, so that he permitted me to come to Munich that I might give them to you.'

" And as he spoke, he drew this from his breast," and my uncle, rising from his chair, went to a desk and took from a drawer a small flat wallet, which I knew at once as the same which my father had given to Daubeney when he left home. " And to my surprise," continued my uncle, " all the papers were there. From which I supposed that Daubeney, fearing some attack, had given the wallet to Bellew for safety, thinking that the man might escape the careful search which the robbers would surely make of his own person."

" But," I cried, " how did this peasant know that Daubeney was a prisoner in the Castle of Czvargas?"

" He went on to tell me," said my uncle, " that shortly after your brother and Bellew had left the house of his mother, she saw a body of men, whom she believed to be a part of the Count's guard, follow the road which they had taken, and that she had heard the sound of firing. And her son learnt that, on the following day, what he took to be these same men had been seen coming from the direction of an inn not far distant from his mother's house, having in their midst a prisoner of great size."

" And did you do nothing?" I cried hotly.

" I did not do much," answered my uncle, " but what I could, I did. I wrote to the Count Czvargas, asking what sum he required for the ransom of your brother. This letter I had secretly conveyed to a house in Spätz, much frequented by the soldiers of the Count, and kept, as I was told, by a 'complice of his."

"Yes! yes!" I exclaimed impatiently, for my uncle was so slow and careful in his speech.

"And I received an answer but yesterday," he said quietly, "for, coming to my office, I found thrust under the door, by whom I could not learn, this paper."

And he took from a drawer a sheet of paper on which, scrawled in a large hand, were the following words :—

"One thousand ducats before the last day of the year, or ——"

And I whistled softly at the largeness of the sum, while my blood ran cold at the sight of that long ink-stroke. But there was hope ; there was still time, and plenty. And yet I wondered at the long respite, and remarked it to my uncle.

"Yes," said he, "it is longer than I expected, but I am told that such is Count Czvargas' custom, hoping that if the ransom money be not found, he may meanwhile have persuaded the prisoner, if he be young and strong, to throw in his lot with his band of ruffians."

"Daubeney would die, rather!" I replied. And then a great wave of furious hatred gathered in my heart for this cruel Count, and a mad desire to beard the ruffian in his Castle took hold of me, so that I rose to my feet on the impulse of the thought.

"Where are you going?" said my uncle, screwing up his eyes at me, as I held out my hand towards him.

"To Castle Czvargas!" I replied.

For a moment he stared at me open-mouthed, and then leaning back in his chair, and throwing back his head, he broke forth into a most immoderate noise of laughing, which filled the room. But I stood sullenly regarding him, my hand held out, resenting his mirth. At length he ceased, but still chuckling, wiped his streaming eyes.

"Oh, you English!" he cried between his chuckles. "You English! What a strange people; and to think that you are my sister's son! And yet, I remember that your mother once, many years ago ——"

But I wanted to hear no stories now, even of my mother, and I broke into his speech with an angry gesture, and once more held out my hand to him. As I stood thus, obstinately silent before him, shamed, but still resolved to carry out my purpose, he said :—

" Tell me again where you are going."

" To Castle Czvargas," I replied, " to seek my brother," and I clenched my teeth, trying not to blush.

" God in Heaven ! " said my uncle, " are you mad, boy ? "

And as I replied nothing, only regarding him sullenly, he went on : " You cannot go ; I say you must not go ! I will send the money that the Count demands."

" I am going," I said.

" How, in the name of the —— ? " began my uncle angrily, but he stopped in time, and I smiled, thinking of how he had checked me for the use of those same words. And then we looked into each other's eyes for a space, silently, until my uncle, placing his hand kindly upon my arm, said quietly :—

" It cannot be done, Nephew, not with an army of men as brave as you. Ah ! yes, I know that you are brave, but this thing that you would do is impossible."

"I shall go, nevertheless," I answered, "and if it be impossible, as you say, I can but come back and ask you for a loan of money for my brother's ransom."

"Loan! a loan of money!" exclaimed my uncle, his cheek flushing with anger, so that I thought the more of him, "do you think that I lend money, I, who have no wife or child, to save my only sister's son from a cruel death?"

"Forgive me, uncle," I said. "I did not mean it. But go I must, and now. I will but look at this Castle Czvargas and return."

"Ah!" said he, "to think that my gentle sister should have two such headstrong sons. Can you not see," he went on, "that by doing this you only keep your brother there the longer?"

And I winced, but was stubborn still.

"He himself would wish me to do it," I said.

"Well, then," said my uncle, "you will at least wait until to-morrow?" And I knew that as he said this he hoped still that he might make me change my purpose.

" Not an hour longer then," I answered. And at that I sat down again, and in a little we went into another room and had some supper, but we were strangely silent as we ate. But afterwards we sat by the fire together, and I talked with him late into the night, telling him all he asked of Wiveliscombe and our life there. And he, on his part, gave me much information of the roads by which I must needs travel, and of the inns and such like ; for though, as I expected, he again attempted to make me stay till he had tried the plan of paying the price asked for Daubeney's release, yet was I determined first to try mine, if indeed my mad desire to see the Castle could be called a plan. And when my uncle bade me " Good-night," I was astonished to think how much and how quickly I had come to esteem this odd, wrinkled, little man.

CHAPTER IV.

I VIEW CASTLE CZVARGAS, AND MEET AN ACQUAINTANCE.

So on the following morning early, armed with my pistol and sword, I rode away; having, by the advice of my uncle, put off the clothes in which I came to Munich, and donned the more sober garb of a student, which he easily procured for me. Even when I was mounted and held forth my hand to bid him Good-bye, my uncle tried once more to make me stay, but I only smiled and shook my head.

As I rode away, I thought of all that he had told me of the Count Czvargas, his cruelty and his love of money; of the sacking of villages by him and his men; and of crimes untold, which filled me with wonder that they should be permitted to go unpunished. And so I rode by Gralzburg and Spätz, and then more warily, until, choosing my time so that

I might the less easily be noticed, I reached, late on an evening, the wayside inn kept by the woman whose son had brought my brother's papers to my uncle.

I found the woman buxom and well-favoured, and as I judged, near upon forty years of age. I had hoped to get from her some information of Count Czvargas or of his following, but she, seeming to be in great fear at the mention of the Count's name, knew nothing, or, if she knew, would not tell me. Only that the Castle lay ten miles distant in an easterly direction, and was easily to be known by reason of the lake in which it stood. The woman, who bade me call her Gretchen, regarded me carefully while I ate the supper which she placed before me, and whenever I would look up from my food I caught her eyeing me curiously, as though she distrusted me, so that I said nothing to her of Daubeney or Bellew ; and had I not my uncle's word of her honesty, I should have feared her, the more so since, after she had shown me to the little chamber where I was to sleep, I heard her quietly shooting the bolt of my door, and, shortly after, talking in a low tone to some other person whose words or voice I could not hear, though I strained my ears to listen. But I was weary with my journey of several days, and before I had lain long I was asleep.

I woke to find the sun shining through the little window upon my face, and dressing hastily, I went to the door, and finding that the bolt had been withdrawn, I passed through into the kitchen. As I did so, my eye fell upon a door which faced me, and I thought I saw the latch move as though some one had gone from the kitchen to this room just as I had left mine, and some one, moreover, who did not wish to be seen by me, or his presence in the house known. I looked from the door to the woman, but she was busy over the fire, and bidding me a surly "Good-morning," she went on with her preparations for my breakfast.

This I ate in silence, and so soon as I had finished, determined to start at once for the Lake Czvargas ; for though only ten miles distant, as the woman had said, I wished to get a good view of the Castle by daylight. The way was easy to find, she told me ; a narrow path leading from the road, through a forest of swamp, almost to the Castle itself.

So when she had given me some bread and meat for my dinner, which I had asked for, saying that I would not return until the evening, I left the house. As I turned out of the road to enter the path which the woman had pointed out to me, being about 200 paces from the inn, I looked back, and saw a figure dart away from the window of the room whose latch I had seen to move when I entered the kitchen. As I looked, the window was shut to, so that I was not able to tell whether it had been the figure of a man or of a woman. Again I thought of treachery, but so eager was I to get on, so as to have a sight of the Castle Czvargas, that I put the fear aside.

I entered the forest by the path, which I found to be so narrow that in many places only one man could pass at a time, and that with difficulty by reason of the thickness of the trees on either side of it. But I made my way along for a distance, as I judged, of four or perhaps five miles, until I came to a place where the way forked into two paths, one of which went a little to the right hand, and the other a little to the left. I had a mind to return to the inn and enquire again of the woman as to which I should take, but supposing that she would not know, and not wishing to waste more time, I boldly chose the right-hand path, trusting that it would bring me where I wished to go.

When I had walked along this path for the space of near an hour, unable to see in what direction I was going, by reason of the denseness of the forest, I came, of a sudden, to a great bog or swamp, in which I was near being caught, sinking in it to my knees, and but for the help of a bough to which I clung, would doubtless have been miserably drowned in mud and slime. But I dragged myself out, and then picking my way with more care, the direction I was forced to take leading me more and more to the south, I slowly, and for many miles, skirted the edge of the swamp, until I was well-nigh spent ; and sitting down, I began to eat my bread and meat. This I found not of much comfort, for I was in a great thirst, and had no water with which I might slake it. So I rose again, and slowly chewing my dinner as I walked along, I once more essayed to get on my way.

And, of a sudden, the swampy ground

ceased, and I found myself upon a hard white road, and before me, with a few thick bushes between, I saw the lake. It took me but a few moments to reach the shore of this, and lying down upon my face, I took in a great draught of water, finding it to be sweet and very cold.

As I rose to my feet, I looked up the lake, and a strange feeling of satisfaction and of dread came to me as I saw, rising out of the water, about five miles distant, the great rock on which was built the Castle Czvargas. Then the thought of Daubeney within it, a helpless prisoner, urged me on to a closer view of it, so that for a time at least I forgot my weary limbs.

Returning, thereupon, to the road, but keeping well to one side of it, so that at the sound of anyone's coming I might seek a hiding-place among the trees, I proceeded upon my way thither. I found that the road traversed the swamp, which was close on either side of it, in a great curve of a half-circle, but whether this was so by nature or by the artifice of man I cannot tell.

When I had gone along this road for near

upon an hour, it touched the lake again as at the southern point where I had first come upon it, and then again curved away with a great half-circle sweep, making the distance to travel by road more than two miles greater than in an even line. From this point I was able to see the Castle more clearly, judging it to be about one mile and a half from where I stood, of which distance I learnt more at a later time. The rock upon which the Castle was built rose sheer out of the water, and from the side of the lake to the rock there stretched a causeway, the nature of which I was minded to examine more closely. So I continued to go carefully along the road, until I saw that I was coming near to the end of the causeway. Here I went more warily, crawling on my hands and knees from one tree to another, but nearly coming to grief by reason of one of my arms going suddenly up to the shoulder in the bog, so that I had almost cried out. But I was rewarded at length by having a very clear sight of the causeway, though my heart fell as I saw the truth of my uncle's words that the Castle was regarded by all who had seen it as being

impregnable. For the causeway (which was
in part rock and in part stone built with infinite
labour on to the rock, and which was a great
wonder to me) went with a gradual slope
upwards to the Castle, being about three-parts
of a mile in length, and was built in such a
way that at its beginning, where it left the
road, it was wide enough to take three horsemen abreast, but as it approached the Castle
it became so narrow as only to allow one
man on horseback at a time, and that, I
thought, with difficulty. And more than this,
the last twenty or thirty yards before coming
to the Castle gate were so steep that I wondered how a horse could carry a man up the
slope; but this, I learnt afterwards, was not
so steep as it looked from where I stood, as
is always the way with a hill before a man
comes to the foot of it.

So that I saw, indeed, that one man with a
pistol or a gun might keep this way against a
hundred, since he would be shielded by the
Castle wall from their assault. I was greatly
impressed by this wonderful sight, and I
ground my teeth in my anger at having come
so far only to find that I was powerless to help

my brother. But yet I determined to try to learn if there were not some way of getting to the Castle from the lake itself, and to this end decided to enter the water at the causeway and to swim right round the rock. But not to-night, for only in the dark could this be attempted, and I knew that on this night the moon would rise too soon after the sun had set to give me time ; and more, my stomach called now upon me to return to the inn for its replenishing.

So, it being now about the hour of four, I turned to go back to the inn, meaning to return on the next night for my wild venture. I had crossed the road into the bushes on the farther side, and had gone forward a few steps, when, on a sudden, I heard the sound of horses coming at the trot, and I plunged in among the trees to hide myself until they should be gone by. In my haste I forgot the bog and sank in it to my thighs.

But there I must wait until these men had passed, which they did soon after, with a great noise of laughing and loud talk, and the clattering of swords and armour. I did not see them, for I was altogether taken up with my own position. I dared not struggle for fear of making a sound that would discover me to the men, and yet I felt my body slowly sinking until I was up to the arm-pits in the filthy slime of this horrible swamp. Unable to wait longer, I caught a thick bough, and with much cracking of the tree and sucking, splashing noise of the mud and water, I dragged myself out, and sat panting upon the bough, my ears strained to learn if I had been heard. But the noise that the men made prevented them from hearing me, and they passed on.

And then I determined upon a course which was like to have cost me my life—though had I returned by the road, as I came, I should likely enough have been taken—namely, to try to make my way across the swamp until I came to the path which led through the forest to the inn.

Watching every step carefully, then, and taking advantage of every tree, sometimes even clambering from one low bough to another, I slowly made my way along. It was as hard a piece of travelling as I ever did; and to add to my troubles I was beset by myriads of small biting insects, which with a thin, buzzing noise attacked my face and hands, causing a sharp, stinging pain and drawing blood. Sometimes I would come upon a small island of firm ground in the midst of this foul mess, and there would I stand and rest until the biting insects drove me on again. I should judge that I had walked and waded and dragged myself along for near upon six miles, my hands torn by thorns, my face covered with blood and sweat, my clothing rent in many places, and my patience and strength well-nigh exhausted, when I once again felt firm ground beneath my feet.

Doubting that this was but another small island such as I had come upon before, but fearing that I should not be able to drag my weary, hungry body through more of this bog, I threw myself down upon the ground, and despite the noxious insects and the cold night air (for the sun had gone down, and the moon wanted near an hour before it would rise), in a few moments I was fast asleep.

When I awoke my limbs were cramped and stiff with cold, and I could hardly move. But, turning over with a groan, I raised myself upon my elbow, and right before me was the most amazing sight that ever met my eyes, simple though it may seem. The sun was up, throwing gleams of warm light through the trees, and making flickering shadows on the grass, and there, sitting before me as though just awakened from sleep, dressed in the uncouth clothing of a peasant boy, a coarse cap covering her head, her large blue eyes looking in wide wonder at me, with something also of shyness, which was very tender and very beautiful to me, was Wilhelmina Skoda. As we gazed, astonished, into each other's eyes, a great wave of colour flooded her face, and then it went so deathly pale that I feared she would swoon away; and yet never a word could I speak. My mouth seemed parched, and I stared helplessly and boorishly at her. At length I found my tongue, but all the use that I could make of it was to blurt out :—

"You! you!" and that was all. But at the sound of my voice, the colour crept slowly back to her face, and glancing down at her strange garb with a shy smile, she said, looking again at me :—

"And you?" Then—and the ways of

women are very strange to me—she buried her face in her hands and fell to weeping most bitterly, so that I felt, did I not do something, I too should blubber like a schoolboy. So I rose stiffly to my feet, and approaching her, touched her lightly on the shoulder, which shook under my hand, but all that I could find to say was: " Fraülein! Fraülein Skoda?"

But she took no heed of me, continuing to cry softly. I was at my wits' end, for never before had I been in so difficult a case ; and then I stammered out :—

" Let us go back to the inn!" For it had come to me suddenly that it was she whom I had seen at the window when I was leaving the inn the morning before.

" Yes, yes," she sobbed, and to my joy she let me take her hands and raise her to her feet. As we walked on side by side (for I now found that we were on the path leading to the inn, at the place where the way forked, which in the darkness I had not known), I racked my brains to find some words of comfort, but none came. The path was very narrow, so that we walked slowly, and I took Wilhelmina's hand, and placing her arm in mine, bade her lean on me. And, as her sobbing lessened, I asked her how it came about that she should have been in the forest at night, alone.

She told me that she had lost her way, and that she would not have left the inn but for the woman, who thought that she would be safer out of doors, and to protect her further had made her put on these strange clothes. And at the mention of them a faint smile broke through the sadness of her face.

"It was you, then," I said, "that I saw at the window?"

"Yes," she answered, "I thought I knew your voice, though you said little enough; but the woman would not let me speak with you, thinking that you were one of Count Czvargas' men."

And then we fell into a silence again, I wondering how I could best ask of her father without paining her, for that some misadventure had come to him, and through this same Count Czvargas, I could see. Yet in spite of her grief and my concern for her, I could not but smile at the odd sight we made. She, graceful and slim for all her uncouth clothing, her gold hair falling from beneath her peasant cap and tumbling about her shoulders in a glistening cloud ; and I, dirty, my clothing rent and thick with mire and slime, my face and hands also smeared with sweat and mud. But I was happy, strangely content in all the turmoil of my mind in the silent loneliness of the deep forest. And I thought of my drinking "Auf Wiedersehen" at our last parting, and looking down at her and at my plight, I laughed. And she, wondering, looked up in my face and smiled, but seeing more than mirth in my look, tried to draw her arm from mine ; but I, placing my hand upon hers, held it fast, pressing it to my side ; and again she smiled, feeling, no doubt at this time that I was in some sort her protector, where she needed one most sorely. It was long again before I felt so content, and I often thought that I should never feel so again. My heart bounded in my throat so that I thought that she must hear it. If she had known how little use was my protection ; if she or I had known how much we were to suffer before —— but that is ever my way ; I cannot keep in the straight path of my story, but must be always harking back and forwards.

And so, mostly in silence, we made our way along the path, which was often so narrow and beset with trees on either hand that I would be forced to lead the way, but even then I would not release her hand. But as we came in sight of the inn, she drew her arm from mine, and I let it go, perforce, wishing that the way had been longer. Frau Gretchen was overjoyed to see Fraülein Skoda again, and astonished beyond measure at seeing the two of us return together. But the maiden pushed by her, and disappeared into her own room, where she hastened, no doubt, to cast off her boy's dress for that which she at least thought became her better ; though I —— : but what matters it what I thought ?

Then, finding myself on a sudden consumed with hunger, for I had tasted nothing since the bread and meat which I had taken with me from the inn, I sat down to the table and ate with great heartiness what was put before me by the smiling Gretchen. And while I ate I pressed the woman with questions of the coming of Fraülein Skoda ; and she told me that the day before my getting to the inn, the maiden had come to her house, tired and footsore, with the story of an attack by Count Czvargas (as the woman supposed) on the merchant train in which her father and she were. She happened, at the time of the attack, being just at the setting of the sun, to be riding with her father in the rear of the party, which, taken by surprise by the sudden and unexpected onslaught of the brigands (for the Count had never before been known to go so far from his Castle in his thieving raids), made but a weak resistance, and Herr Skoda had cried to her to dismount and hide among the bushes until he came back for her. This she had done, trembling with fear at the firing of the guns and the noise of fighting ; and there she had remained, shivering with the cold, for many hours, until, fearing that the worst that could had happened to her father, she had stolen away, and, scarce knowing what she did, wandered without hope through the forest. All that night and the next day she had spent in vainly trying to find her way, until at last, when scarce able to drag her feet along, by a glad chance she saw the light in this woman's house.

"She came to me bravely enough," said

Frau Gretchen, "though worn and haggard with her weary night and day, for God knows there are few honest resting-houses so near the Castle Czvargas" (and so great was the woman's fear of him, that she cast a look of dread behind her as she spoke the Count's name), "and me he only leaves in peace that he may be able to get my only son for one of his soldiers. So I took the maiden in," she went on, "and put her to bed. And when you came, sir, I feared that you might have been sent to spy upon me, for who knows who may be trusted in these bad times?" And the woman fell to whimpering.

But I had had enough pain to keep my darling from weeping already, so I just left her to her tears and went into my room. Here, after trying in vain to rid my clothing of the mud and slime which covered it, I cast myself down upon my bed, for I was still stiff and weary from the doings of the past day and night, and while I thought of what was still before me to be done, and listened for the return of Fraülein Skoda to the kitchen, I fell asleep.

CHAPTER V.

HOW I ENTERED CASTLE CZVARGAS.

WHEN I awoke with a guilty start of fear that I should be too late for my work at the Castle, I was pleased to find that the time was not yet much past noon. Settling my disordered clothing as well as I could, I entered the kitchen and sat down at the table, while the good woman placed upon it a smoking meal, for which, strangely enough, I felt myself quite ready. Then going to the door of Fraülein Skoda's room, the woman called her, and she, coming in presently, sat down beside me.

I could still see the marks of her late tears upon her face, but as she took her seat she gave me a shy glance that made my cheeks burn with pleasure.

" To-day is my birthday," she said.

" And mine," I answered, scarce knowing what I said, " was on the first day that I met you in Venice" (though my mother would have said that it was not for two full months yet). At that Wilhelmina blushed deeply and most prettily, her eyelids fluttering as they went over her eyes, so that I thought she knew the meaning of my words.

She was now dressed as I had seen her first, but more simply, as for travelling on horseback, and her gold hair was, after the quaint fashion of German maids, put into two long plaits which went below her waist. We said little during our dinner, for in some way (though we spoke in English, which she could not understand) the presence of the woman constrained us. But afterwards we talked of our last meeting, and how, if I failed to find some means of helping Daubeney I should return, and together we should make our way back to Munich. This was the first that she had heard of my brother being prisoner to the Count Czvargas, and I could see that she was much concerned by the intelligence ; but she tried to keep me from going into useless danger. But at this last I laughed, wishing, I fear me, to seem braver in my lady's eyes than in truth I really was. And that I did not lessen the dread in which she held the Count was very plain to see.

So, then, I dallied with the time until the hour at which I meant to start ; and as I bade Wilhelmina " Good-bye," I smiled with all the show of hopefulness I could, and went away quickly, lest the wistful look in her eyes should draw me from my purpose. As I turned again to look at her, she waved her hand to me, and called in a voice from which she could not altogether take the tremor of her tears, " Auf Wiedersehen," and I smiled the dear words back to her.

And never before that day had the turf seemed to me to spring so softly, nor my feet felt so light and my spirits more gay, so that as I strode along I bellowed catches of my favourite songs, and then laughed again to think that these were all of war and fighting and of deeds of valour, and never a word of the love which was surging in my heart. And, indeed, it seemed to me then that the venture I was upon could only bring success, for failure was so far away from my thoughts, as my lady's blue eyes and rippling hair of gold danced before my lover's sight, and the rustling forest trees made whispering echoes of "Auf Wiedersehen"; so that I found myself hurrying on my way that I might the quicker return to meet the eager welcome in her face; and in my conceit I laughed aloud, and could scarce keep my feet from running. But, in truth, there was another look in her dear eyes when next I looked into them,—and in mine too.

When I came to the forking of the ways, I was careful to take the left-hand path, and in a short while I found myself upon the road near to the place where it met the causeway leading to the castle ; so that I thought that all the time in which I had been struggling through the quagmire the night before I was scarce twenty yards from the forest path.

The sun was setting when I came here, so I was content to wait within the shelter of the trees until it was quite dark. Then I lost no time, for I had scarce two hours for my task, and stripping off my clothes, I crept cautiously upon the road ; and coming from the darkness of the forest to the white, open road under the sudden clearness of the starlight sky, and the clear open stretch of water gleaming away to the distance, it seemed very light to me.   But I slipped quickly across the road and into the lake on the northern side of the causeway, but could scarce keep from gasping at the coldness of the water.   But when I began to swim I felt less afraid, and went quickly and quietly with a long breast-stroke, keeping as close to the causeway as I could ; for if I were seen I might give myself up as dead ; and so I came to the great rock upon which the Castle Czvargas was built. But my heart sank as I looked up at the side of this, rising sheer and smooth above me, with not a crack or cranny that would hold one's fingers.   But I went on, swimming slowly and easily, the cold water nipping my blood, until I had gone all round the rock, and came again to the causeway, on its southern side.   And when I reached this spot I had well-nigh revealed myself, for here there was a boat tied to an iron ring driven into the rock, from which a rough flight of steps led up the sloping side of the causeway to the castle gate, and in the darkness of the water my arm struck the boat with a clear sound. But this was not heard, and so I swam back as quickly as I dared, with but that knowledge of the boat, and one thing more, which was so little that it scarce seemed possible that it could ever be of any use to me. For as I had swum round the rock, I had come upon a place, at its most eastern point, where there was driven into the rock a strong iron ring, just like the one by which the boat was fixed, and near it a small shelf of rock projecting under the water (against which I cut my hand), and large enough for one man to stand upon. I climbed easily to this, and searched the surface of the rock for any show of steps, but it was smooth and polished, with no sign of any way of getting up; though I could dimly see that at the top the castle walls, which rose straight up all round, showed a break here, where, I should judge, before the causeway had been made it was the custom to get to and from the Castle. The boat and this, and a great fear of being seen from the Castle, and a frozen body, were all that I had of comfort for my pains, as, under the faint light of a rising moon, I found my clothing, and as fast as I was able, with chattering teeth and trembling limbs, I put it on. Then,

with one more look at the Castle standing grim
and terrible in the moon's pale light, shaking
my clenched fist at it and its owner's hateful
power, I plunged into the forest with the
thought of how soon I could convey Fraülein
Skoda back to Munich, and bring Daubeney's
ransom-money to Count Czvargas.

So that when I came to the place where
the paths forked, my body was warmer, and
my heart was filling with the glad thought
of the welcome waiting for me at the inn.
And then, suddenly, I heard a sound behind
me, and before I had time to turn or draw my
sword, I felt a heavy blow come crashing on
my head, and I fell senseless to the ground.

When I opened my eyes again, and looked
about me with a strange dizziness of my sight
and a fearful soreness of my head, I saw,
standing over me, a ruffianly-looking soldier
who held a pistol pointed at me, and when
I moved, I found that my arms were bound
tightly to my sides, and my feet together.
As I tried to rise, the brigand struck me
cruelly in the face, and with a low German
oath bade me lie still. This I did, perforce,
a great sound buzzing in my head ; and when

I opened my eyes again the trees seemed to move ever in circles in the faint, chill light of the early dawn; by which I knew (for my senses were becoming something clearer) that I had been in a swoon for many hours.

Presently two other men came to us, and one of them quickly undoing my legs bade me get up and march, kicking me roughly to hasten me. I rose heavily to my feet, and would have fallen by reason of the swimming of my head, but for the support of the strong arm of one of the men, on which I leant until the giddiness had in some measure passed.

"But," I said stupidly, as the men showed me that I must go back in the direction that I had so lately come,—"But I am under promise to return to Fraülein Skoda!"

"Donnerretter!" answered one of them. "Get on, march!" and then with a coarse laugh he added: "I promise that we will not take you far from the fair maiden!"

And I, dimly wondering what his words might mean, took the path behind one of the men, the two others following me. We went slowly, for I was only able to stumble along with pain and difficulty, despite the brutal thrusts of a sword with which the soldier who came next to me tried to hasten my steps. How I was able to travel those weary miles I know not. Escape was impossible, had I even had the sense to think of it ; for I was hemmed in on each hand by the dense forest, and with my arms bound to my sides, I knew that a step or two on either side of the path would take me to my death in the foul morass. But I had no thought of escape, only a numb despair and weak anger at my carelessness, and a growing hatred for the power of the Count Czvargas into whose hands I knew that I was being taken.

And my faltering mind wandered causelessly from one thought to another. The steady tramp of the soldiers' feet, the jingle and rattle of their spurs and armour, and the hateful buzzing of the biting insects, seemed to burn into my throbbing brain as I tried to think of Daubeney, of Wilhelmina, and of my mother. And I smiled feebly at finding myself stupidly wondering what was the story of my mother which my uncle had been going to tell me when I stopped him, and to which I had given no thought until this moment.

At length, after blundering along for what seemed hours to me, we came upon the road which I already knew so well; and the fresh air from the water striking my face brought me to a better sense of my position as I followed the man before me, and looked at him more knowingly. He was a strong, thick man, wearing a helmet from which there hung a black plume, and a cuirass of steel, and long boots reaching to the middle of his thighs, with great spurs that jingled and clinked as he walked. He was armed, as were his two companions, with pistols and a long sword.

Without so much as a glance behind, he crossed the road on to the causeway, I after him, the two others closing up so as to walk on either side of me. And so we walked until we came to the Castle gate. Here a great impulse beset me to cast myself into the water and to drown miserably, or be shot, rather than be taken into the presence of the Count. But life is sweet, and hope clings fast to the heart so long as life lasts; so I stood and waited for what might follow.

The soldier who went in front, whom the others called Karl, and who alone had not shown me any unkindness, knocked noisily at the iron gate, and at the sound, a small slit, made by sliding a thin shutter on the inside, revealed the mouth of a pistol, and a man's voice asked who came.   And Karl answered in a loud voice :—

"We, Karl, and Fritz, and Friederich!"

"Give the word, then," cried the other. And in a loud voice Karl spoke again :—

"Himmel, Himmel, Himmel!" he said; and I remember that I felt how strange a word it was to gain my entrance to this place. At the word the gate was slowly drawn open, and we passed inside.   Then the gate clanged to behind us, the heavy iron bolts were shot again into their places, and, with a shudder, I knew that I was a prisoner.

So this was the way in which I entered the Castle Czvargas, after all my foolish hopes and boastings, and my fine exploring of the lake.

CHAPTER VI.

COUNT CZVARGAS.

THE man Karl left me standing with the two others, and passed through a door in a wall on the right-hand side. While we waited, I cast curious looks about me. On my left hand, close within the gate, I saw a small room in which were sitting two men whom I took to be the sentinel-guard, a third walking constantly backwards and forwards before the gate, now and then stopping to peer through the grille. On the right hand was a high stone wall without window or other opening except the door through which Karl had gone; and in front of me, for some ten yards, between high walls, leading from the gate, there ran a passage-way opening into a court-yard, across which I could see men passing.

I had but time to note these things, wondering the while in what part of this huge Castle Daubeney might be, when Karl

came back, and telling the other two that
they might go, himself led me through the
same door on the right into a long dark
passage from which many doors opened on
either side.   At the end of this passage we
came to a door in the wall which faced us.
Here the soldier knocked, and at the sound
of a harsh voice bidding us enter, he lifted
the latch, and holding me by the arm, led me,
bound and with my head bursting with its
throbbing pain, into the presence of Count
Czvargas.

For he it doubtless was.   He was reclining
easily upon a settle by the fire, having lately
finished his breakfast, the remains of which
lay on a table before him ; in his hand he
held a great tankard which he drained as we
came in.   He was the swarthiest man that
I have ever seen.   His face was bronzed so
that it looked in colour like an ancient copper
coin ; a tangled mass of black hair covered
his head, and a coarse, black bea d his face
up to the eyes ; and these were of the
blackest, with a strange, dull glea.n in them,
which, over-shadowed as they were by thick,
black eyebrows, gave him a sinister appear-

ance. He was, I judged, near forty years old, and might have been thought a handsome man but for his mouth, for the thick growth of hair that almost covered it yet failed to hide the red coarseness of the loose, wet lips; and when he grinned (for I could not think he ever smiled with such a mouth), he showed a row of small, stained, broken teeth, and a line of bright red gum like an animal's. His hands were large and strong, and thick with the same black hair; and so was his breast, which I could see in part by reason of the openness of his shirt—a very Esau of a man, as I thought, regarding him.

He looked me up and down as though I had been a noxious beast, and I turned red under his glance of open scorn. For I was like to feel humbled at this way of meeting Count Czvargas after my boy's talk with my uncle, and my proud desire to seem brave in the eyes of Fraülein Skoda. He regarded me long, his look filling me with a sullen, helpless rage, and then he asked my name.

"Franc;," I said, and stopped, for in a moment it came to me that I had best not reveal to him that I was Daubeney's brother.

"Francis?" he said, and looked at me keenly, while for all that I wanted it so much no other name would come to my troubled mind.

"Francis," he said again, and then I knew that in his ignorance of English he concluded this to be my surname.

"Your country?" he snapped.

"England," I replied as shortly; and he looked curiously at me, whilst I thought that he might be surprised that Daubeney and I should understand the German tongue so well.

"What, then, are you doing here, in my country?" he asked.

"I was on my way to Munich," I answered—as indeed I was when I was taken.

"Rich?" he sneered, and I saw that he regarded the humble style of my soiled dress, so I merely shrugged my shoulders.

At that he threw himself back upon the settle, and bidding Karl go, he and I were left alone, facing each other, with the table between us. He lay back on the settle, one hand under his head, the other hanging down and toying with some object on the floor, while he regarded me cunningly out of the corners of his black eyes. But my eyes, following the movement of his hand, had caught sight of the object which he toyed with, and at this I stared, wondering. Ah, how well I knew it! For it was the Belt which I had won for wrestling and given to Daubeney at our parting; and a mist came to my eyes at the thought of the last time that I had seen it. And Count Czvargas' eyes slowly went with mine until they too lit upon the Belt. This he lifted up, and then looked curiously from it to me and to my waist, where his eyes fastened upon Daubeney's Belt, which I was wearing, the silver shield of which was revealed by the disorder of my dress.

"God in Heaven!" he cried, "this boy has one too! Do all you English wear them?" and, rising, he came towards me, and roughly unfastening the buckle, dragged the Belt from my waist. He looked closely at it, and from it to the other, and then again to me.

"What are these?" he asked.

"Belts," I answered; and for a moment he glared in fury at me; then, with all his force, he swung the Belts and struck me across the face with them, and the sharp edge of one of the shields caught my cheek with a stinging pain, and I could feel the blood trickling down my neck. But I was glad that I had not winced or moved, only that I had shut my eyes; and whether this loss of blood cleared my head, or the suddenness of the blow I cannot tell, but the pain and throbbing left it for a time.

"You fool!" the count hissed at me, his face glowering with passion close to mine, "you stupid, baby fool! But what are these?" and with a snarl of rage that showed his gums, he held the silver shields close to my eyes.

But before I could answer him, there came a knocking at the door, and Count Czvargas, stepping back from me, called in an angry voice who was there? At this Karl entered, and going near to him spoke some words in so low a tone that I could not catch them. But I saw, as he listened, that the flush of passion passed from his face, and in its stead there came a look of satisfaction that I liked no better. Waving his hand as a sign to Karl to remove me, without so much as a glance at me, he threw himself on the settle again, and fell to curling his black moustaches with an ugly leer on his dark face. And as I turned to follow Karl, I had a strange sinking of the heart, wondering what this sudden change in the Count's manner might mean.

Beckoning to me to follow him, Karl led the way back to the passage leading from the gate, and fro there to the courtyard, and across that (the men who saw us idly regarding me) to a small room at the eastern side of the Castle, near the stables. Directing me to enter, the man closed and bolted the door upon me, and I found myself alone. Alone with my thoughts. And there was not much comfort in them ; for now there seemed no hope of any sort for Daubeney and me but that distant one of succour from our uncle's purse.

My eyes had not been idle as I crossed the courtyard, but all I saw served only to increase my sense of helplessness. The Castle buildings went all round the courtyard except at the most eastern point of the rock, where there was a narrow opening which, as I had judged before, had once been the entrance to the

Castle from the lake.   Had I been alone and unbound I might have thought to fling myself into the water at this place, but of what use were such thoughts now?

I was not left alone for long, however; for in a few minutes Karl returned bringing with him the great hulking soldier whom he called Fritz, the same that had used his sword-point to urge me faster on my painful way to the Castle.   First they loosed my arms, and the freed blood ran through my numb hands with tingling pain.   Then they stripped me to the skin, even making me remove my boots and hose, and as they closely looked at each garment, they threw it back to me to put on again, and I was thankful for their quickness, for the room was cold.   But they found nothing, for the reason that I had left what money I had for the journey at Frau Gretchen's house, and of papers I had none.

The different way in which the two men treated me was very marked; Fritz handled me most roughly, cursing at the job; while Karl was gentle, regarding me, I thought, with a sort of careless pity.   But when I gave a hasty glance into his face, with a sudden throb of hope that I might have one friend in all this host of ruffian thieves, he would not meet my look. Even then I hoped that if he came to me alone I might somehow learn that he was friendly; but when he came, as he did presently, bringing me some coarse food, he said not a word, but placed the platter and a cup of water on the ground, and left me wondering and uncheered.

The cell was cold and dark, being lighted only by three narrow slits high up in the wall; there was no chair or couch, and the rock floor made a most hard bed. I ate the food, which Karl had brought, with little relish, though I drank the water eagerly, and then, curling myself up into a corner, I fell into a troubled sleep. As I tossed to and fro, my mind went back to Fraülein Skoda, and with a suddenness that brought the pain throbbing to my aching head, I knew that the soldiers who had taken me had found me only by chance, while on their way to or from Frau Gretchen's house; the rough words of the man that I should not be taken far from Fraülein Skoda, and the message that Karl brought which caused Count Czvargas to leer and plume himself—ah, yes! all these meant but one thing, that she, too, had fallen into the hands of the cruel Count. For me and Daubeney death might come, that was the worst, but for her ——? Then I think that the wound of my head and all the troubles through which my mind had been, brought on some kind of sickness, for I remember nothing of the two days that followed, coming to my senses to find Karl giving me some strong broth with a spoon. At the sight of him, I smiled foolishly, and when I tried to get to my feet I wondered to find how all my strength had left me, and was glad enough to sit down again before the giddiness of my head had caused me to fall.

But during the days that followed my strength returned quickly, and even some new feeling of hope, for, to my astonishment, a rough sort of care was taken of me by the man Karl, so that I was even allowed by him to sit at the door of my cell, and to bask in the warm sunshine. But, save when I was shut up in the cell, he was ever at my side, keeping guard, so that had I even had any thought of trying to escape, it would have been impossible. But I had no thought of it, knowing as I did how closely the gate was watched ; and as for the opening to the lake, though I believed that a desperate man might cast himself from the rock into the water, and, by swimming, get to the shore, yet would he be surely taken again if he were able to get so far.

On the first day that I was allowed to sit outside my cell, I was struck by the quietness of the Castle, seeing only two or three men, and only one at a time, walking in the court-yard. And at first Karl would answer nothing to my questioning, sitting or standing by my side in moody silence, as though he did not hear me speak. But, one day, I asked him suddenly, as we sat at the door of my cell, how many men were left to guard the Castle while the Count was away on an expedition. And he had answered " Four," surprised himself, I thought, at having spoken. And I, in my turn, was startled at his reply. Yet not more than four were needed, for even one might keep the gate alone. But it set me thinking again, hopelessly of my position, and of Daubeney's and Fraülein Skoda's ; and at thought of her my cheeks would burn with anger at my foolishness in coming to the Castle as I did, when, had I been more wise and less eager to seem a brave man to her, I might have safely guided her back to Munich at the first, and so saved her and me from being taken by the Count. Then I would think of his cruel face and shudder at the thought.

But I was to obtain an assurance of his loathsome cruelty which should render me more hopeless still. One day, as I sat with Karl, we heard the noisy sound of horsemen coming to the Castle, and though Karl hastily put me in my cell, and closed the door, I could hear that the men had returned, as, with a great noise they came riding into the court-yard. The next day I was not allowed to sit outside, and saw Karl only when he came in with my food (which though coarse, was yet in plenty), until the afternoon, when he came to me and told me that I was to go outside. Wondering what it might mean, I followed him, and stood, as he bade me, against the wall. And I saw that all, or nearly all the soldiers, about forty in number, were standing round the courtyard in groups of two or three, and that Count Czvargas was seated at the farther end. But it was towards the centre of the courtyard that my eyes went; and there I saw two men, strong, lusty peasants, facing each other, armed with swords. As I looked they began to fight, clumsily and awkwardly (so that the soldiers laughed and jeered at them), but with so earnest a purpose that I knew it was not only a show to them, as it was to the others. They cut furiously at each other, lunging and darting back with fierce, outlandish cries, their eyes flashing hatred and fear, their breath coming noisily.

But it could not be for long, for one of the men was longer in the arm and quicker than the other, and as I watched them, my own breath coming fast at this my first sight of fight to the death, my hands powerless to stop the brutal sight, I saw the weaker one receive a slashing blow which glanced down the side of his head, shearing off his ear and a great piece of skin and hair, and landing with a horrible force upon his shoulder, so that he fell under it. The other, in his fierce desire to live (for this I learnt afterwards from

Karl was the prize of victory) would have plunged his sword into the breast of the fallen man, had not a loud shout from the Count called him to stay his hand. And at a signal from him, two men, accustomed to the work, came forward and bound the arms of the miserable wretch who grovelled on the ground and shrieked for mercy—bound them close to his sides. The Count then spoke something to the other peasant, pointing to the lake; but he drew back, shuddering; but the Count threatening him, he stooped, and lifting the struggling wretch, took him and flung him from the rock into the lake below. Ah, me! to think that I should stand and see such devilish cruelty and yet be helpless to avenge it. I can hear the horrid splash and muffled screams of that poor victim now. . . .

As the Count walked back from seeing his fiendish purpose carried out, an ugly grin on his black face, he glanced maliciously at me, and bade Karl put me back into my cell. And I was glad to be alone. But I would not wish for any one, however bad he were, to pass through such an hour as I did then. I think that I went mad with passion, hatred and despair. I shouted curses on the Count, crying and sobbing in my rage, striking my helpless hands against the stone walls of my cell so that they bled. And yet, I thank God that, looking back upon it now, I had but little regard for my own life, but of Daubeney I thought, and Fraülein Skoda, and our home in peaceful Wiveliscombe.

After a while my passion spent itself, and when Karl entered with my food, he found me lying on the floor, sobbing like a child. But at his coming I sat up and asked him fiercely when my turn would come. But he only looked at me in surprise, and shrugged his shoulders.

For I knew that this was why the Count had made me stand and watch the fight between these prisoners, that I might know what he held in store for me. And I wondered what I should do when the time came (though I knew I could not come to any hurt by the clumsy peasant's sword); if I were to die I hoped that I might not add to the foul Count's gloating joy by showing fear or cowardice.

But though I had heard the sounds as of

another fight after I had returned to my cell, and had wondered dumbly if Daubeney had been made to view it, I was left alone that day.

CHAPTER VII.

OF COUNT CZVARGAS' ELOQUENCE; AND OF MY MEETING WITH DAUBENEY.

BUT the next morning Karl came to me and said that I must come into the presence of the Count; and I followed him, wondering what it might mean.

Count Czvargas was standing before a great wood fire as we entered his room, and for some moments he looked keenly at me without speaking.

" Do you know one Daubeney Nutcombe?" he said at length, and I started at the suddenness of his question.

"Yes," I stammered. And he grinned and looked me up and down, slowly, as though measuring my strength, while I did the same to him. To his advantage; for in size and figure he resembled Daubeney so much, that, as he turned to kick a fallen log into its place, I marvelled at the likeness. But the faces!

I could see my brother's dreamy, blue eyes, his fair, curling hair, his pink cheeks and thin, firm lips—and then this one turned his hateful black face upon me with its ugly grin.

"You can use a sword?" he asked me.

"A little," I replied.

"And can you wrestle, too?" he said.

"I can do a little of that, too," I answered. And he laughed a jarring laugh.

"Well, we shall see," he said; and I wondered what he meant.

"Which Belt is yours?" he asked me, and as he spoke he turned, and taking the Belts from where they hung against the wall, threw them on the table. Without thinking, I took the one which I had been wearing when I came to the Castle.

"This," I said.

"For sword-play?" the count asked shortly.

"Yes," I answered, trembling lest Daubeney had given a truer answer, for that the Count had asked my brother I saw in that he knew that the Belts were for sword-play and for wrestling. But he went on.

"This Daubeney Nutcombe," he said, "can he beat you at the wrestling?"

" He has beaten me often," I replied.

" Well, we shall see!" he said again; and now I knew what he meant.

Then Count Czvargas' mood seemed to change and the look of his face; and after regarding me quietly for some minutes, he began to speak. Slowly at first, and in a soft voice, moving his hands before him as I have seen a preacher, but afterwards eagerly and with violent gesture. And as I listened to him in open wonder, it came to me that this was his weakness, his vanity of speech; and doubtless he made much use of this strange power over the ignorant men who served him. I think it pleased him to see the wonder in my face, for he spoke thus a full hour or more, holding me with the force and eloquence of his words.

Of his early youth in Germany; and wrongs that he had suffered; of crimes ascribed to him but done by others; of duels and battles wherein he had shown bravery and prowess; of this Castle, and the causeway he had built; of the beauty of his country and the lake; the ease of life and its enjoyments; of his train of soldiers bound to him by love and interest; of their pleasant life of freedom and of comfort; of sudden goings out by night and the return laden with rich spoil; and I caught his meaning, shuddering at the thought that he should want me to join his ruffian band and help in his devilish warfare against unarmed men and helpless women; but he went on in careful, telling words, so that had I but heard his voice I might have been tempted to believe his lies; but when I looked into his cruel face, his loose lips mouthing out these bribes, a foul froth dribbling on his coarse, black beard, I loathed him so that I had much ado to keep from dashing my fist in his vile face.

Then suddenly his voice changed to a harsh note of menace, and he spoke of Death; by sword or gun when unprepared and sleeping; by a dagger in the dark; by equal combat in the courtyard, as I had already seen; by horrible drowning with arms bound. Then he ceased, watching me keenly from his black eyes; and without another word waved his hand to Karl to remove me, and we left his presence, Karl stolid and silent as ever, my mind filled with amazement at this odd show. But as we reached my cell I turned to Karl and said :—

" His Excellency the Count likes much the sound of Count Czvargas' voice." And the man grinned at my attempt at pleasantry.

And after that, for some reason, he was less silent when I spoke to him, answering my questions shortly and gruffly, but still answering them, and this I felt was something gained. But not much. For now I knew that the Count's purpose was that Daubeney and I should face each other and make a show of wrestling and of sword-play for his men ; and the conditions of the match ?—the winner to kill the other ? I laughed grimly at the thought of the Count's rage when either of us should refuse to do his cruel bidding.

But there was not much occasion to laugh, the outlook was bad enough. I racked my brains day and night for some loophole of hope of escape, but nothing came to me ; and day after day passed and yet no further prospect of the end. This I saw was by reason of the Count's absence from the Castle upon some expedition, which was of some advantage to me, in that I was, as before, allowed to sit out in the sun during the day. Wondering what had become of the peasant who had slain the other in the combat I had witnessed, I asked Karl what had been done with him.

"His victory won him freedom," said Karl, "but only because he could not fight."

I need not say that, finding Karl more friendly, I tried to learn from him some news of Daubeney, but he would tell me nothing, feigning ignorance; nothing but that so far as he knew Count Czvargas had not questioned him as he had me, but only addressed him in the same way.

But one day, the day before that of which I must now tell you, I asked Karl if he had any brothers, thinking of my own.

"I had two," he answered, his face flushing (as I thought) with anger.

"Are they both dead?" I asked, feeling sorry for him as I spoke.

"Yes!" he said with bitterness, looking away from me, "murdered both, and by the devil Count!"

I was taken aback by this unexpected

answer, but I put my hand on his arm and stayed him from leaving me, as he was about to do.

" The other prisoner is my only brother," I cried. But he only stared stupidly at me, and shaking off my hand, went away before I could say more. And so I gained nothing from telling him, only the fear that he might tell the Count. Yet even if he did, what could it matter now? only that the Count would take a keener delight in the unnatural fight. But I misjudged him, for the next morning he was more kind to me than usual, and told me that this was the day fixed on by Count Czvargas for our display of English wrestling.

" And who wins," he said, " must slay the other, so they say ; but how, I cannot tell, like enough by casting in the lake, as you have seen."

And the man left me, while I held my head between my hands and groaned. Both of us to die ; for I knew that Daubeney would die himself a thousand times before he hurt me. Both! All because that I, in headstrong folly, had chosen to refuse my uncle's wise advice.   And I threw myself down in a very torment of remorse and of despair.

To-day!   A few hours and it would be over.   Daubeney and I would both be dead ; and Fraülein Skoda—but at the thought of her sad face and wistful eyes, and of all that might come to her if this foul man should have his wish, I sprang to my feet and cried aloud in my mad, helpless rage that no power on earth should kill me so long as she was in his treacherous grasp.   No power on earth?   I laughed horribly at the grim nonsense that I raved.

And then it came to me, came like a lightning-flash, burning into my maddened brain, so that I stood glaring wildly with wide eyes at the blank wall in front of me, seeing nothing but my plan.   My plan?—yes, mine!   I might still try it, if only I could have a word with Daubeney.   If ——

But as I thought it the hope went; for Karl entered at the moment and told me that I was to come with him into the courtyard. I opened my mouth to speak to him, but with a frown he stopped me, and led the way out of the cell.   And at the door the Count stood

watching us. That he must have seen something of the trouble in my face was certain,
but without a word he turned and walked
towards the opening in the Castle walls, Karl
and I following ; and pointing down at the
dark water, he spoke to me again of Death,
much as he had before, but, I thought, with
greater force. Then, regarding me silently
for a few moments, he turned on his heel and
went away, leaving Karl to take me back to
the cell.

What could this mean ? I thought. Why
should Count Czvargas wish so much to
impress on me the fear of Death? Only I
think that, when the time came, I might fight
more fiercely for my life for the better show
to him and his men ; and also that he might
have an occasion to show his power over me,
and his eloquence. But if indeed death was
to come to me, I vowed that I would let this
man see how an Englishman could face it.
And with a great desire to have it over, my
chance or not, I paced my narrow cell in a
very fever of excitement ; the time passed so
slowly that I feared something had come to
stay the contest. At every sound of passing

footsteps I would stand and wait, expecting Karl; and at last he came, and opening the door bade me follow him, which, with beating heart, I did. But only just outside the cell, where he signed to me to stand.

Escape? The very carelessness with which the men regarded me showed how impossible that was. Many of them were lounging about, and, as I came out, glanced up at me, and then resumed their work or talk as though I were nothing; as, indeed, I was to them. And as I saw this it seemed to me that what I called my plan was but child's play: so slight a chance it was, so trivial a trick. Yet I clung stubbornly to it. Rather fail so than die cruelly at the Count's hands. And again I thought that Wilhelmina would remain behind even if Daubeney and I went free; only for a time, I thought, only for so short a time that Count Czvargas could not hurt her in it!

When I had stood thus for a few moments, looking hopelessly round, I heard, approaching from a passage-way near where we stood, the steady tramp of men, step for step. But I would not look in the direction of the sound, fearing that Daubeney might be one of them, and that, by recognising me, he would spoil all. For I wished to warn him by a look or word before he should have time to call out in his surprise; so I stiffened myself as closely as I could to the wall, trying to hide myself behind Karl's great body, until the men should come near enough for my purpose. But I could not do it. One soldier, armed, walked before my brother, and then he came, and after him another soldier, great men all. And I smiled to think that Daubeney's size, and perhaps some show of strength when he was first taken, made the Count regard him as more worth watching than me; and I was proud of him, my brother, as I peered from behind Karl and watched him coming.

He held his head high and looked before him with a calm indifference that compared oddly with the strained look of anxiousness which I felt upon my own face. But, suddenly, he caught sight of me, and all the indifference passed from his face like a breath of wind. Taking a quick step towards me with out-stretched arms (and they were cruelly bound with cords), in a great voice of strange joy and grief he cried my name, " Frank!"

And the warning I had meant to give him was choked from my throat by a great gulp, and my eyes, which should have told him to be silent, were thick with tears.

One of his guards, looking curiously from him to me, took him roughly by the arm, and made him stand against the wall, himself taking up his position in front of Daubeney, the other soldier on his right hand, and Karl between us brothers. But I felt Daubeney's eyes upon me as I looked straight in front of me, trying to disregard his wondering gaze.

The afternoon sun blazed down upon the courtyard with its groups of men idly waiting for the show ; a dog barked, a horse stamped, a man laughed ; and we stood there in fateful silence, while my heart beat loudly in my ears. But I could not bear the feel of Daubeney's questioning eyes upon me, and I turned to Karl, and in a husky whisper (for my lips were dry), said :—

" For the love of God, Karl, and the memory of your dead brothers, let me have a word with mine!" And I saw that the man was moved, and I went on: "Only one word, Karl, before we die as your own brothers did, one last word before the cruel Czvargas kills us!" And I think my eyes pleaded with him more eagerly than my voice.

" I will try," he said, and for a moment or two did nothing ; and every moment meant so much ; the Count would soon be here.

" Fritz!" said Karl, at length, to the soldier on Daubeney's right, whom I knew again as him who had treated me most brutally when I was being taken a prisoner, " Go tell his Excellency that all is ready." I saw that the man hesitated, but with a jealous look at Karl, he went, muttering to himself. As he went Karl stepped forward and spoke to the soldier in front, leaving Daubeney and me with none between us. I wasted no time.

" Dubs!" I said, and at the sound of his name there came a strange break in my voice, and a pitiful look in his eyes, "listen to me! I have a plan. You and I are known to each other, but my name is Francis ; do you understand?" And he nodded, and I went on hurriedly, for Karl looked round at us : " We

are to wrestle, you and I, and who loses dies ;
I must lose.   I, do you hear me?"   But my
brother slowly shook his head, looking sadly
at me, and I knew that he thought I wished
to sacrifice myself for him, as, in truth, God
knows, I was ready to do, if it were needful.
"Who lives matters little!" I cried, and then
I stopped, for Karl hastily stepping back to
his place between us, pushed us apart, and
looking up, we saw the Count entering the
courtyard.

CHAPTER VIII.

I TRY MY PLAN OF ESCAPE.

THE Count and some one else. I knew who it would be before I saw her face, but Daubeney could not have known, for at the sight of her he uttered a great cry of wonder and of rage. So that for a moment the eyes of the men were turned from the Count and Fraülein Skoda to him. But only for a moment—such a sight as we made was common enough, but never one of them had seen anything so beautiful or pure as my dear lady.

Was ever man in so great a turmoil of troublous thought as I was then? And yet I had to stand, holding myself back, or spoil it all. Count Czvargas was leading the maiden by the hand, and as, coming into the courtyard, she looked up and saw the crew of ruffian soldiers staring rudely at her, she shrank back for one moment; then, drawing herself up, and plucking her hand from the Count's, she walked bravely to the seat which had been placed for her beside his. And my whole heart went out towards her in a great throb of pity, love and wonder at her brave show. Glancing at Daubeney, I saw in his face a gleam of such wild rage as I had never seen there before, and feared that in the suddenness of his anger he would do something which would make us lose our chance. But, with a sob of powerlessness, he looked down at his bound hands and then at me, and his eyes were full.

Count Czvargas, with a look of satisfaction and of admiration, which, though I hated him the more for it, seemed to me to take something of the cruelty and evil from his face, followed Fraülein Skoda as she went to her seat, and bowing low before her so that his long black plume touched the ground, sat down at her side.

She sat, her hands clasped tightly together, with her eyes upon the ground, and the Count, regarding her in open admiration for a moment, then looking up towards Daubeney and me, beckoned to our guards to bring us to him.

As we reached his presence, she, doubtless expecting to see two peasants or the like, glanced timidly up at us, her eyes travelling quickly from Daubeney to me, a look of such terror and despair coming into them, and a great catch of pain in her breath, that I went hot under it ; and then her face went deathly pale, so that I thought she must swoon away. Not thinking of my act, I stepped forward to support her, as I thought to see her fall, but Count Czvargas, with a muttered oath and a buffet of his hand, stayed me, looking anxiously again at Fraülein Skoda. But as, with one hand to her side, as though her heart pained her, she bravely sat upright beside him, his eyes turned to me with such a look of scowling hate that I almost cowered under it.

"You dog!" he cried, "you wretched English dog! to cast your ugly looks upon my lady. Get you gone!" and with an angry gesture he bade the guards take Daubeney and me farther back.

But I was glad that now he hated me the more, since it made what little hope I had for Daubeney greater. At a word from the Count, who was still watching Fraülein Skoda

with a care which she at least liked little, one
of the men went away and presently returned
with Frau Gretchen, the good woman of the
inn ; and I was pleased at sight of her, for I
felt that Wilhelmina had at least this friendly
woman as a companion, and in some sort a
protection.

Then Count Czvargas addressed us ; spoke
as he had before spoken to me in his room,
but in a loud voice that rang across the courtyard, and could easily be heard at the farthest
end.   No doubt he wished to show some of
his eloquence to Fraülein Skoda, and to look
well before her in this way, and perhaps also
to us, and to impress his men.   But as for me,
I blessed him for his vanity of speech ; for it
meant delay, and delay until daylight had
faded was what I wished for most.

I cannot tell you much of what he said, for
my mind was too filled with the turmoil of my
hopes and fears—hopes for Daubeney and
myself, and fears for Fraülein Skoda.   My
face must have shown the Count that I was
not listening, for suddenly I was startled by
his shout of " Listen, boy! Listen, if you
wish to live !" and, looking up, I saw that he

was frowning angrily at me. But he went on, and I watched him, listening to his words, but gathering little sense. And one of the soldiers, standing near him, yawned ; with a snarl of rage he stopped and called to him to come forward, and when he came, without a word, he struck him such a blow upon the head that he fell like a log, and was dragged away by two others of the men.

But Fraülein Skoda shrank away from him, shuddering at his brutal strength. One of the soldiers, then, at a word from Count Czvargas, came forward and loosed the cords that bound my brother's wrists, and the Count told us to begin.

This much of his speech I had understood, what I already knew ; that Daubeney and I must show our English wrestling, and that he who was beaten died. I knew also that Count Czvargas hoped that it would fall to me to die, as he believed that Daubeney had won the Wrestling Belt, and, as I had told him, had often thrown me in a wrestle. And I wished that it should be so ; but more ; or else my plan were quite of no avail. The conqueror —what was he to gain ? Freedom, I hoped ;

though could scarce believe that the Count's treacherous face would grant so much. But unless that were the guerdon of the victor, what use to go on with this sham? Yet what else was there for us to do, to try? For Karl had told me that to make his prisoners fight the more fiercely for his pleasure in the sight, Count Czvargas would sometimes offer free-dom to him who killed the other. But what he meant by freedom I did not learn till later.

When we had gone some twenty paces from the Count, he called to us to stand. So we removed our boots and coats and stood before each other. Then we shook each other by the hand, and some of the men laughed. But I was glad that these all stood idly by the walls, none being near enough to hear us if we spoke; and the grasp of Daubeney's hand in mine brought a new courage to my heart.

How I looked, I know not; but God knows I felt anxious; and in Daubeney's face there was a look of dread resolve that made me fear he would not act the part I had laid out for him. But, as we wheeled about each other for the catch, I cried to him in a low voice : " Let me win this bout, but make it long !" And so we caught each other with an equal grip, and feigned to try and make a throw ; but it was ill feigned, and I feared that the Count would not be deceived, so, suddenly, I drove my hip under Daubeney's, and turning quickly jerked him over my back on to the stones. I wished these had been turf, as, no doubt, did he ; but the suddenness of my act surprised Count Czvargas and the soldiers, and they were silent.

I was facing the Count as I stood, and I looked at Fraülein Skoda, and saw that she was watching us with frightened eyes. As my look met hers, her eyelids fluttered, and her face went pale, as I doubt not that she wondered what would be the outcome of our contest.

As Daubeney rose to his feet, I saw with satisfaction that the sun was sinking fast ; but half an hour was wanting yet before it should set. So we faced each other again, and I, having turned, so that my back was to the Count, whispered to Daubeney :—

" A long, fierce bout, and I must win again !" and, his perplexed face showing that he did not trust me yet, I sprang at him, gripping him tight, and cried :—

"Trust me, Dubs! I have a plan, and you must help me. Think that our mother is watching us, and *play*." And he shivered in my arms at the mention of our mother, but he understood me.   For often, when at home, to tease our mother, who always thought that we must kill each other in our sport, we would feign to wrestle with the utmost fierceness, as though in anger, until, in her distress, she would run to us and try to tear us apart ; and we would laugh and tell her it was only " play."

So for a long time we wrestled, feigning to be in anger, and that we deceived all those who watched us was plain to see. Our eyes flashing and our teeth clenched, our breath coming and going noisily, first one and then the other of us appearing to gain some advantage.   But at last, at a sign from me, using my favourite throw (which had helped me to win the Wrestling Belt) I cast him on his side. That I should win I saw was pleasing to the men, but with Count Czvargas quite otherwise.   He frowned, gnawing his black moustache, and cried aloud, taunting Daubeney :—

"What of the Belt?" he said, "the Champion Wrestling Belt? Are you not shamed to let so small a man beat you, a giant? Why, I could throw him with one hand!"

"Come, then, and try!" said Daubeney under his breath; and I was pleased to see this spirit in him. But the Count went on :—

"Look you!" he said, "he who wins goes free to-day; free to leave the Castle, and go where he pleases. He who loses dies. Once more!"

And I rejoiced, yet not too hopefully; for the harsh anger of his voice, and the look of cruel treachery on his face made me feel that though he would be too sure to keep that part of his promise which brought about my death, yet would he not relish letting Daubeney go free. But that was all I had to hope, and on that I must, perforce, rely.

So I rose to my feet, and going towards Daubeney, who still lay where he had fallen on the ground, I touched him with my foot as though spurning him in contempt. At that he rose and faced me, a look of anguish on his face; for he could not tell what I was at. So I gripped him close once more and whispered :—

"Wrestle so that we get near the opening to the lake; then 'break my back'!" And Daubeney caught something of my plan, and as he always used at home, did as I told him. So that as we flung each other to one side and the other, slowly he drove me back, until we were within ten paces of the opening. Then I loosed my hold, and as though by weakness, let him get the under catch.

"Now!" I cried. And as I write this, I see it all before me; the great courtyard, surrounded by the Castle walls, grim and strong, the setting sun throwing dark shadows across; the soldiers watching now with keenest interest the struggle between us; the Count, glancing ever and anon at Fraülein Skoda at his side, but regarding us with angry eyes; and she, gazing at us brothers, of whose love towards each other she so well knew, fighting for life, as it appeared to her—she gazing fearful, and wondering. And Daubeney, towering above me with a questioning, dread look in his blue eyes, thinking yet that

I was sacrificing my life so that his freedom might be gained. But he trusted me; and yet I wonder that he did; for as he bent me back and back, I struggled fiercely against his overwhelming weight and strength, twining my legs round his in seeming weak endeavour to keep him from doing that which I wished him to do. Planting my feet upon the ground, I strained, or seemed to strain against his crushing power; but still he bent me back and back, until at length, with a great cry as if of pain, I fell down at his feet, with his questioning, fearful face bending over, close to mine.

"Tell him my back is broken," I had just time to say. "When you are freed, keep close to the shore and look for me. If we do not meet I will return to Munich with all haste." It was a long speech, but I meant it to be my last, for as I finished speaking, some men came up towards us. Then I lay still, wondering how I could make my legs look helpless. For I remembered seeing a man once, long ago, whose back was broken by a fall of earth, and who was quite sensible and strong in the upper part of his body and

his arms, but his legs were useless, and they
had told me he was paralysed.   Presently the
Count came up to us, and with a coarse laugh,
struck me cruelly in the side with his foot;
but I lay still, feigning to be unable to move,
one leg doubled painfully up under me.
Calling then to two of the men, he bade them
bind my arms; my legs he let go loose, as
I had most hoped, because they looked so
powerless, and, as I believe, that my dying
struggles might be the more prolonged.

"He will win no more Belts for baby sword-
play," he said ; and, turning to Daubeney, he
went on : "You did well to throw him at the
last, and yet I thought the little man would
beat you.   Now, finish him!" and he pointed
to the lake.   And Daubeney, with heavy
steps came towards me, and stooping, lifted
me tenderly in his great arms, his body
trembling, and his breath coming in great
sobs of dread, the sweat pouring from his
face.

"My God, be quick!" I cried, as if in
torment, though I thought that only Daubeney
could understand my words.   But one other
heard them ; for as Daubeney, with his giant's

strength, lifted me up above his head, and I closed my eyes waiting to be cast, we heard a woman's cry of " Mercy!" and for a moment he stood, balancing me in his arms; and then they fell, and he let me to the ground.

What we saw was this. Lying grovelling on the ground before Count Czvargas, her white hands clinging to his feet, was Wilhelmina Skoda, pleading for my life. Ah, my love! I thought that I had loved you well before; what could I say of my love now, seeing you lying there at that brute's feet, pleading for me? And yet, thank God, I had the strength to bear it all, and lie quite still; but what a great strain it was upon me, no man can ever know. And what Daubeney may have felt I cannot think, when, turning her face to him, her lovely face down which the tears were coursing, she cried in angry pain :—

"You, you! How can you ever hope to see your mother's face and tell her this? Can it be true, oh, can it be true that you are his brother?"

She spoke in English, but I trembled lest her angry flow of words should tell the Count more than I wished him to know. And a great flush came to his cheeks, and for a moment he hesitated, looking down into my lady's tender, beseeching eyes, as if the appeal in them touched even him ; but, in a deep silence from all who looked, the only sound being Wilhelmina's sobs, he stooped and gently removing her hands from his feet, signed to Frau Gretchen to take the maiden away. When these two had gone, the Count turned with an oath to Daubeney, and was about to tell him to get done with it, when a fresh stir occurred, a soldier coming in haste to the Count and speaking some words in his ear. He listened eagerly, and seeming to forget about me for the moment, walked a few paces off, calling to Daubeney to come with him, leaving me lying there, wondering what would be done to me.

But every minute made it darker, and I did not mind so it was done. And presently I heard the Count cry out an order, and Fritz came towards the group of soldiers who were standing silently beside me. With a horrid grin, he said that " His Excellency " had bid him cast me into the lake. And I think that each man there was glad that Fritz and not himself had been ordered to the task.

As for Fritz, he seemed to take a pleasure in it, even smiling with a grim content as he lifted me up and held me in his arms. But I hung limp and helpless, catching my breath, until I felt his body give a great heave and the muscles of his arms go hard with the strain of my weight; then I closed my eyes tight, and the next moment he had sent me hurtling through the cold, dark air.

CHAPTER IX.

A COLD SWIM, A SHORT SLEEP, AND A GREAT SURPRISE.

NOT more than three beats of a man's pulse could have been counted before I touched the water, but to me the time seemed long. I ground my teeth as I rushed through the air, and I struck the water with a resounding splash and a smack that caused so sharp and stinging a pain, that I thought I had struck against the rock. All the great breath of air that I had taken was driven from my body by the blow, and I had much ado to keep under the water long enough for my purpose ; and more than this, I could not know for certain in which direction I should go to reach the rock. But I struck out blindly with my legs, so that at the moment that my head rose above the surface, it came against the rock most sorely, giving me almost as much pain as joy.

As I rose, I gave a great cry of distress—
and it was not wholly feigned—and of relief.
Relief? Yes, in truth! for though my hands
were still bound to my sides, I knew that if I
could but get upon the shelf of rock (of which
I had learnt when I swam first in the lake,
thinking it then of little value to me), I might
get free, and so my plan, such as it was, might
stand some chance of being safely accomplished. For some minutes I stayed where I
was, treading the cold water with my feet,
until I became more used to my condition and
the dim light; then slowly I made my way
along the rock, keeping close against it, until
with my body I felt the rough shelf I looked
for. But on this I found it more difficult to
seat myself than I had thought. I turned my
back to it, and driving my feet down with all
my force, I tried to jerk my body on to it;
and thrice I failed, but the fourth time I sat
upon its very edge, and by striking furiously
with my feet, I was able to keep my seat, and
slowly get more secure upon it, hoping the
while that the noise I made would not be
heard, or if it were, that it might be only
thought to be caused by my drowning

struggles. I strained my ears to catch the sound of any movement in the Castle above, but heard none.

And so I sat, shivering with the cold, waiting until the darkness was more safe. My shirt was split open with the force of my meeting the water, so that my breeches and my hose were all the clothes I had. My first task was to loose the cords which bound my arms to my sides, and, though I had wished it a task less painful, it was well that I had some work to do while I sat shivering there, for it brought some warmth to my body. But struggle as I would (and my perilous position prevented me from moving much) I could not loose the rope. As I leaned back against the rock, to ease the cutting pain of the sharp cords before I strained against their strength again, I felt a sharp point that pricked my shoulder ; and I had, perforce, to try to cut the rope through with this. And I did it at length by a constant tedious moving to and fro and up and down, with many a near approach to falling from my seat, and a scoring of my arms with cuts that stung and bled. By the time that I had freed my arms,

my body ached with the awkwardness of my
position, and I hardly knew if I had feet and
legs, to so great a coldness did the water
numb them. I bound the rope about my
waist by way of a belt, and taking off my
shirt, which, in its rent condition, would but
clog my arms, I chafed my wrists and body
into a semblance of some warmth.

By this it was quite dark enough for my
venture, and I dared not wait longer for fear
the moon should rise, which I knew would be
within the hour. So I slipped quietly into the
water, and struck out for the right-hand shore,
directing my course so as to reach the bank
as near as might be to the spot where the
road from the Castle came first upon the lake,
and where I hoped, if indeed he were let free,
I might meet my brother Daubeney.

At first I swam as a dog swims, with my
arms below me, and only my head above the
water, for quietness' sake and for warmth also,
seeing that the distance was not like to weary
me. But presently I went more boldly, with
a long, sweeping breast-stroke that took me
through the water pleasantly, and I began to
feel warmer ; and as my body warmed, my

spirits rose bringing a glow of hope to my mind. I found that a slow current which set towards the south of the lake helped me a little, so that in about three-parts of an hour I felt the ground with my feet, and though I was still near a score of yards from the bank I gladly let my body down, and finding the water to my shoulders, I began to walk slowly to the shore. Then, suddenly, I heard a sound which brought my heart jumping to my mouth with a new fear—the sound of voices and the splash of oars. That I had not heard them before was a marvel to me, and crouching lower in the water, I turned and looked in the direction from whence they came. At first I saw nothing, but in a moment or two I caught the glimmer of a light stealing round a projection of the bank ; this I saw came from a lantern in the front part of a boat. I had no doubt it was the boat from the Castle, and I stood so that my head only was above the surface, and waited. The boat came slowly towards me, and now I heard the voices of the men who manned it.

" Here," said one, " we had best land and walk ; my body is frozen with the cold air."

"Yes," said another, swearing softly, "let us get this devil's errand done, and back to bed."

But I paid little heed to what they said, only that I thought I knew the sullen voice of him who spoke the last, as I stood and watched the light come steadily in my direction. I dared not move, but cowered there, shivering with cold and fear, my eyes fixed on the lantern, which with each stroke of the oars seemed to leap nearer to my face. And so I remained, trembling, but thankful for my black head of hair in that its likeness of hue to that of the water helped me from being seen, until at the next stroke the sharp curve of the boat's bow would have struck my face; then, taking a great breath of air, I drew my head under the surface, and tried to crouch down upon the bottom of the lake. Now this may seem an easy thing to do. But it was not. For the great breath of air that I had taken made my body very light, so that, do what I could, I found myself rising slowly to the top, and fearing lest I should come against the boat, I was forced to swim lustily, striking out with my arms and feet to keep me down.

And even as I did this one of my feet lightly touched the boat, and in my terror at the feel of it, I gasped, taking in a great gulp of icy water that went near to choking me.

When my face came to the surface (and I could not have stayed under the water for another moment), it was all that I could do to keep from making a great noise of spluttering. But for that same breath of air which I took then I was most thankful, for I was like to have burst had I not got it at the moment. My eyes opened wide to learn where the boat was, and I was expecting that I myself would surely be seen; but the noise that the men were making kept them from hearing me. For as I looked, I saw that the boat was drawn up to the shore, and the two men who had been rowing threw down their oars with a clattering noise. Then one held the lantern up while he who had been steering (who I thought had complained of the cold) stepped out, and tied the boat by a rope to a tree root, and then stood beating his body with his arms to get them warm (while my teeth chattered in my head) while the other two also got to land. And then the three of them walked off briskly down the road leading towards the south.

For some time I could see the twinkling of the lantern as it swung in the man's hand, and not till two full, cold minutes had passed after I had lost sight of the light, did I venture to come from the water. As I slowly and cautiously made my way to the point where the boat was tied, there came a thin, faint streak of light over the lake, and looking up, I saw the moon rising beyond the eastern mountains. Cowering lower, dragging my feet through the thick mud of the lake's bottom, I crept under the shadow of the boat, and my eyes coming to the level of its side, fell upon that which filled me with delight— a great thick cloak which promised some warmth and comfort to my frozen body, and which he who had steered had evidently worn and thrown off so that he might not be encumbered by it as he walked. The boat was too deep to let me reach the cloak from where I stood, waist-deep, so that I clambered in, and snatching it up, gladly wrapped it about me.

Then a sudden thought came to me, which,

but for the cold which dulled my senses should have come to me when first I saw the empty boat. Now I flung down the cloak, and leaping out, untied the boat from the tree root, and giving a great push with my foot, leaped in again and, once more wrapping the good grey cloak around me, I waited to see where I would drift; finding, as I hoped, that the lake current took me slowly towards its southern end. I dared not use the oars for fear of being heard, or even of being seen by the men who had but just now left it, or from the Castle, which seemed very near to me as I saw it standing out clear in the moonlight. For the moon was rising in a cloudless sky, lighting up the surface of the water with great brilliance, so that at any other time I might have wondered at the beauty of the sight. But now I was content to lie at the bottom of the boat, and to pray that the moon's light might not reveal me to my enemies.

And as I lay there, thinking of the men whose boat I had taken, the words that one of them had spoken came back to my mind. "This devil's errand."—Devil's errand?

repeating these words to myself until with a dull pain it came to me that Daubeney was the object of their search, they having doubtless come so far by boat so as to avoid the great curve of the road and to get more quickly on the way which my brother had taken, having most likely seen that he went in that direction. Freedom? This then was what Count Czvargas meant! and I cursed him softly under my breath.

But there was some hope yet; for if my belief were true Daubeney was still free, and might even now elude the search of his pursuers, one of whom at least seemed to like his task little. But if they should come upon him, and take him, as they easily could, seeing that they were armed and he had nothing with which he could defend himself, what should I do then? I could but try to make my way back to Munich to my uncle's; for no search would be made after me, a drowned man, as they thought.

With such poor comfort I was fain to lie in what patience I might, and wait. And now, though the cloak was yielding me some pleasant warmth, a great feeling of hunger

beset me ; and all that I could do to stave off
this sense of emptiness was to tighten the
rope about my waist, and this extra tightness
had to do instead of the more pleasant feeling
of a plenteous pressure from within.   Then,
wondering idly where Daubeney would be
by this, and how and where he and I might
next meet, my thoughts leaped to Fraülein
Skoda and the horror of her position (though,
indeed, her face had been constantly in my
mind), and then to Daubeney again and my
own case, until I think I dozed, helped by
the silence of the night and the warm cloak.
And it was no wonder, for my mind had had
much exercise that day, and my body.

How long I slept I know not, but I awoke
suddenly in great fear, with the sound in my
ears of arms cleaving the water and the noisy
breathing of a tired swimmer.   It was so close
to me that I dared not look over the side of
the boat, but drew myself up a little, and
dragging one of the oars quietly to me, I
raised it so that I might use it as a weapon of
defence.   And so I waited and listened to the
swimmer as he slowly and with evident labour
came nearer, the noise he made telling me

that he was well-nigh spent. Then I heard the gentle rubbing of his hands against the boat's side, and an eager cry of relief as he clutched its edge. But I had no room in my mind for pity, as I brought the oar smartly down upon his knuckles; and yet it gave me little pleasure to do the cowardly act, as with a cry of anger and despair the man let go his hold and disappeared. It was useless to try to conceal myself longer, so I sprang up, and holding the oar poised over my shoulder, waited for the man's head to reappear, brutally stifling my feelings of tenderness with the knowledge that only so could my own safety be secured. As his head came to the surface I struck hard at it. But something, the heartlessness of my act or the rocking movement of the boat as I sprang up to strike, unsteadied and weakened the blow, so that the oar glanced from his head to his shoulder, driving him again beneath the water. But as he rose once more, and I had lifted my arms to strike with more purpose and effect, he uttered a great cry of despair, flinging his hands up; and I, with a new fear and hope rushing through me, stooped and peered into the shadow for a sight of him. The next moment I had flung my oar clattering noisily into the boat and was reaching over the side in frantic effort to clutch the drowning man before he sank again ; for the glimpse of his face showed me Daubeney, my brother, whom, in my ignorance, I had been so cruelly striking to his death.

My fingers twined in his fair locks, and with much labour and rocking of the boat I was able to drag him to the stern, and there, by using all my strength to draw him up and into the boat, though in the doing of it his giant's body received some sore bumps and bruises. After I had chafed his hands and limbs for a minute, I was gladdened by the sight of his opening eyes. But when I saw the look of dreaming wonder in them as they quietly closed again, I fell on my knees beside him and wept like a child. For I had been filled with the awful dread of having done my own brother to death, and even though it might have been in ignorance, yet would it have taken from me all desire to live.

But he, coming back to life, regarded me with a strange smile, and feebly asked me where we were. While I fussed over him like a mother over her child, until his senses returning, he was able to sit up and look around him. In a few minutes we were both recovered enough to take the oars and pull at them with all our remaining strength. But, in truth, this was not great; for Daubeney was much exhausted by all through which he had gone, and I, though something rested by my short sleep, was not in much better case. Moreover, neither he nor I was skilled in the handling of a boat, having had but little practice of the kind. So that we could not do very well, but we did all we could. And it was better than sitting still and waiting for the drift to take us. The exercise warmed us, where we needed warmth much, for all our clumsy efforts, and brought a glow of hope to us that lying idle could not have done, and we became quite cheery at the thought of being free once more.

We said little, speaking only in whispers, and pulling stoutly at the oars. I thought, as I need not say, of Fraülein Skoda, wondering how soon we might help her; but at the present each moment was of so much value to us for our own escape (without which being secure we could be of little use to her), that we must wait until we were more surely free from the danger of being again captured before we formed fresh plans. And we almost forgot the weariness and distress through which we had passed in our great desire to get ever farther from the hateful clutches of Count Czvargas and his prison Castle. But I knew that we had yet to pass the point where the road touched the south extremity of the lake (where I had been so glad to slake my thirst on the first day that I came there) before the three men who were following after Daubeney. We, in the boat, had the shorter distance to travel, but how much start they may have had, how long I had slept, I could not tell. And I felt sure that knowing Daubeney could but keep along the road, they would follow it, and fast, so that they might keep warm. Once past this spot we should be safe, for a time at least, and could then afford to take some needed rest. Also I wondered when next we should get a good meal, my stomach calling loud to me for satisfaction.

But now a new difficulty arose to hinder us. We had been feeling that with each stroke of our oars we came so much nearer to safety, when we found our progress stayed by a curious swirl of cross currents, which, despite our efforts (they being but feeble in the weary state of our bodies) took us towards the shore. Finding this, we stopped rowing, trusting that the current would lessen, or, after it had taken us near the bank, help us again on our way. And so it was, for when we came so near as almost to touch the shelving side, our course was once more slowly southwards.

As we took the oars again into our hands, Daubeney turned to me and said :—

" Have you given any thought to the poor girl —— ? "

But I stopped him with an exclamation of alarm, and looking up we saw that which seemed to imperil our own safety. We were just at the very point where the roadway touched the lake's side, and coming along the road, so near, that in a minute they could not fail to see us, were the three men whom we so much wished to avoid, one of them carrying the lantern, which now gleamed dimly in the moon's bright light. To hesitate for a moment meant to be seen and taken, for in the open moonlight on the water we could not fail to be noticed ; so I cried in a whisper to Daubeney to get ashore among the bushes with all haste.

CHAPTER X.

HOW WE ENTERED CASTLE CZVARGAS
A SECOND TIME.

AND we were just in time. Not waiting to tie up the boat, we had but managed to scramble on the bank, each of us taking an oar as our only possible weapon, and to crawl under the shadow of a thick bush, not daring to go far in by reason of the softness of the ground, when we heard the voices of the men, grumbling still at having to be out on so cold a night. With beating hearts we listened, scarce daring to breathe, as the steady tramp of their heavy feet and the creaking swing of the lantern came nearer and ever nearer to our hiding-place. Then we saw the faint flickering lantern light, as the men came within three feet of us, and, turning with the road walked briskly on away from the lake. And then, as we began to breathe again, at the one moment when I would have wished it not to come, I sneezed.

I was lying behind Daubeney, and at the noise I made, he looked round quickly at me with so odd an expression on his face, that, before I knew it, I had burst into a great peal of cackling laughter, which broke strangely upon the silence of the night. And I stopped as suddenly as I began, and peered through the bushes at the men. They were standing still in the middle of the road, with looks of fear upon their faces, one clutching the other by the arm. For a full minute they stood thus, we two watching them in silence and wonder. At last they turned and began to step slowly towards us, he who carried the lantern coming last, lagging behind the others.

As the foremost of the men reached the other side of the thick bush in whose shadow we were lying, the boat grated with a long harsh sound against the bank. The men started at the sudden noise, and one of them cried out. But this was a more natural sound than those which I had made, and, recovering from their fear, they went on towards the lake. There they saw the boat which they themselves had left tied up two miles away,

and one of them stooped and catching the line
which hung from the boat's bows, tied it to a
tree, remarking as he did so that the oars were
gone. At that we saw them turn again
towards our hiding-place, and we knew that
they now thought my sneeze and foolish
laughter to be no spirit sound, but to have
come from the "devil of an Englishman"
whom they were seeking. As for Daubeney
and me, we knew that all was lost unless we
took them by surprise. But it was little
chance ; for we had only clumsy oars for
weapons, while they, we saw, had swords and
pistols. But they were only three against us
two, and one of them, more frightened than the
rest, still lagged a pace or two behind, bearing
the lantern. If only we had swords, I thought,
we might show them, or Daubeney might,
how we had learnt to use them.

Now we could feel the men beating the
bushes with the flat of their swords, as they
cautiously advanced, two being on Daubeney's
side of the bush and one on mine. Then
Daubeney started up with a great cry and
struck the first soldier a terrific blow upon the
head which sent him crashing to the ground,

dead, with a broken skull.   And as he fell, my brother snatched the sword from the man's right hand (the left had held a pistol which, in his surprise, he had not fired), and rushing at the other hurled himself upon him with such a sudden violence that, unable to defend himself, and burdened with the lantern, he fell without a groan, the sword going right through his chest.

At the same moment that Daubeney had risen, I leapt up and made a blow at the soldier nearest me.   But in my eagerness I misjudged the distance, and the oar-handle struck down the man's arm just as he pulled the trigger of his pistol, which was pointed at my face.   The pistol exploded, and I could feel the bullet whistling about my feet.   I did not give him time to use his sword, but, dropping the oar, I flung myself at his waist, and gripping him close, I threw him easily to the ground ; so easily indeed that I wondered at his weak resistance.   As we fell together, I left my hold of his body and clutched his throat with all my strength, trying to strangle him ; and again I wondered that he did not struggle against me, his hands grasping the grass at his sides ; but then, for the first time I saw his face (for his back had been towards the moon which shone upon me) and I saw that his eyes were starting from his head with a great horror of surprise ; and I myself was amazed, for the man was Karl, my friendly gaoler, Karl. As I saw this, Daubeney came rushing to my aid, and raising the sword from which the warm blood of the slain man dripped, he would have plunged it into Karl's body, had I not checked him.

"Kill him, kill him, Frank!" he cried in so strange a breathless voice that I looked up, to see him standing with upraised arm, and in his maddened eyes the hateful lust of war.

"No, no!" I cried in haste, "'tis Karl!" and I was scarce in time, for Daubeney in his madness, his face ugly with the desire to kill, had almost given the fatal thrust. But at my word he let fall his arm, looking at us blankly as though he did not see us. And I loosened my grip of Karl's throat, and saw the look of horror slowly passing from his eyes, as he hoarsely muttered :—

"Ah, my God ! you are not dead ; you are not drowned !"

"No!" I answered with a grim smile, "I am not dead or drowned, nor is my back broken.   I am no naked spirit of the grave to which Count Czvargas thought to send me; but look you," I went on, "there is no time for talk; will you befriend us? Will you help my brother and me to escape?   In my excitement I had closed my hands upon his throat again, and his only answer was a choking moan. So I let go his throat, and roughly shaking him by the shoulder, cried again :—

"Will you help us cheat the Count, your master?"

"The Count?" the man replied, "my master?   He is no master of mine!" and he turned his head to spit on the ground.

"Will you help us, then?" I cried. "Come, man, be quick and answer me!"

"Yes," he said, and I let him rise. "Yes," he repeated, gazing at me with a kind of stupid awe, "I will help you, if you need help; but no power on earth can ever kill you now."

And I laughed at his surprise that I had escaped the death to which the Count had thought to send me; and my laugh did more than my words to make him feel that I was really flesh and blood. But yet he shrank a little when, calling to Daubeney to bring the oars, I took his arm and led him to the boat. I looked round as I spoke, and saw my brother, still with the sword in his hand, standing and looking down at the soldiers whom he had killed. Then a great shudder went through his body, and he covered his face with his hands as though he would shut out the sight of them, the sword dropping to the ground, and glinting red in the moonlight.

Seeing that he was like to give way to the feelings which had hold of him, I ran back, and picking up the oars, touched him roughly on the shoulder, and called to him to come on. For I was fretting at the delay; the moon was giving so bright a light, and every moment meant so much to us. And Daubeney turned and came stumbling after me, staring out over the water with a strange far-away look in his eyes. As we reached the boat, Karl, looking from Daubeney to me in a stupid way, said, as though he had no other thought but this :—

" He is no master of mine! But a devil

from Hell!" and again he spat on the ground with a contempt and hatred which no feeble words of mine can convey. But I stamped my foot, and shook him by the arm, thinking the while that I had two strange companions in our danger. They got into the boat as though asleep, and I, unfastening the rope, followed them.

"Which way?" I asked of Karl, and he pointed down towards where a stream opened from the lake. Taking my seat, I thrust one of the oars into his hands, and told him to row with me. So we proceeded for some time in silence, keeping near the shore, drifting with the current more than by our efforts at the oars. Then the silence was broken by Karl muttering softly :—

"He is no master of mine!" and he spat into the water. And his oft-repeated words, the anxiety, the excitement, the haste and the relief after our great danger all acting upon me in a strange way, I broke out into a weak, foolish laughter that I could not stop. But the other two looked blankly at me, Karl turning to do so, and said nothing ; and after a while my laughing ceased, leaving me weak and ashamed of my weakness. So we drifted on in silence again, until we had passed down the stream for half a mile. Then a strange thought came to me, and I asked Daubeney, not knowing how much his answer was to mean to all of us :—

"Why did Count Czvargas call you to him?"

"Why?" said Daubeney stupidly, seeming to be half asleep, though I had no surprise at his understanding what I asked, "he wished me to join him on a raid. . . . He ——"

"Was that the message the man brought?" I cried, breaking in upon his speech.

"It was," said Daubeney shortly.

"And did he go—the Count?" I cried.

"He did," said my brother; "he took me with him to the gate, and 'since you will not come with me,' he said, 'Auf Wiedersehen!'"

"How many men did he take?" I cried to Karl, clutching his arm.

"All," said he, "but two, and those two others and me," and he nodded towards where we had left the two men lying.

"My God!" I shouted, "tell me, when will he be back?"

"That would be hard to say," said Karl slowly, and I cursed him for that same slowness; "if he meet with the train and get the spoil, he would be gone three days ——"

" But if," I said—and I had stood up and was leaning over Karl in my eagerness—" but if he failed ? "

" He should be back in a few hours from now," he drawled.

And then I sprang back to my place, and drove my oar into the water with all my strength, so that I turned the boat to the bank.

"Pull in !" I cried hoarsely, "pull in !" and I could hardly speak, for my mouth went of a sudden dry in my excitement. In a moment the boat struck the shore with a shock that nearly took us from our seats.

"Get out !" I shouted (as I thought, though afterwards they told me that I only whispered), and as I spoke I leaped ashore and tied up the boat.

" Where are you going, Frank ? " said my brother in a quiet voice that angered me ; so I shook him roughly, putting my hands to his shoulders, and speaking with difficulty.

"Going?" I sobbed; "to the Castle, do you hear? to the Castle, man, to rescue Fraülein Skoda before the Count returns!"

That woke him up, as I knew it would, though it was the first he knew of my knowing the maiden's name. But I did not wait to see, but plunged through the bushes on the way back to the road. The way was bad, the ground giving under my steps in many places—and Daubeney from his weight had more difficulty even than I—but I scrambled on, and in a few minutes reached the good road. Looking back I saw my brother toiling on behind me, and Karl struggling a few yards back.

"Come on!" I cried, "come on!" And I began to run. So great was my excitement, that I was able to run for the greater part of a mile, but then a sudden weakness came over me, of hunger and of weariness, and I stopped, panting, with my hand to my side. And Daubeney and Karl came lumbering up together after me, my brother pale and breathing hard. Karl was the best off, for he was fresher, and had boots and clothes; but I was naked to the waist, for in my eager haste I had thrown off the cloak with which I wrapped myself when in the boat; and my stocking soles and Daubeney's were rent and worn with our scrambling through the bushes and the hard road; for Daubeney had removed his boots when he swam out to the boat. But I did not feel the cold, nor did I know how torn and sore my feet were, for my mind was surging with the wild hope of saving Wilhelmina.

When the other two came up to me, I started on again, in a heavy, plodding trot, my mind going ever faster than my body; but every now and then I would, unknowing, break into a quicker run, and stop again, and pant for breath until the others caught me. Never were eight longer miles, never a sight more welcome to two tired men than the Castle Czvargas and its causeway when, at weary length, we came to it. But we shuffled on, sobbing in our hurry and exhaustion, the last half-mile taking us full ten minutes. As we neared the gates I told Karl what to do, which I had planned as we were coming.

Thereupon he went to the gate and

knocked loudly upon it, while we waited anxiously for the sentinel's voice. He must have been asleep, for some moments passed without an answer from him, and not till Karl had knocked again more loudly did he ask "who went?" And Karl answered, as I had told him, and not too truthfully, I fear :—

"I, Karl, and Hans, and the English prisoner with us!"

"Give the word, then, and let me get back to the fire!" was the sleepy reply of the man. And by this, and his tardiness, we knew what we wished most to know, that Count Czvargas had not returned, else had he not dared to be . so careless at his post, trusting to the noise which the body of horsemen would make to give him warning of their coming. But Karl cried the word, thrice, as I had heard him before, and I burned with a fresh pang of jealous anger as my lady's name rang out from his unknowing lips, in the still night: "Wilhelmina, Wilhelmina, Wilhelmina!" and I wondered how Count Czvargas had come to know it.

Then we heard the sleepy sentinel slowly

draw the bolts, and as the gate heavily opened for us, Karl asked if His Excellency had returned, to which the other simply answered, "No!" Karl, then, taking Daubeney by the arm, pushed him before him, my brother holding his hands behind him as though they had been bound; and I followed close on Karl, keeping his body between the guard and me. Then the gate closed behind us, and the guard, without even looking at me, too careless to ask where the third soldier was of the three who went to capture Daubeney, turned to go back to the warm fire. So that my sudden attack upon him easily brought him to the ground; and there, with Karl's help, I held him while Daubeney found a cord wherewith to bind his arms and legs; nor had he yet recovered from his astonishment when this was done. The other man, who was quietly sleeping on the guard-room floor, was as easily secured.

So, for the time at least, my brother Daubeney and I, with Karl, were in possession of Castle Czvargas.

CHAPTER XI.

A STORMING RAGE, AND A PEACEFUL REST.

But we did not want to possess the Castle, rather we wished to get away from it with as much speed as possible. So leaving Karl to guard the gate with Daubeney, I passed through the door on the right, and going to one of the rooms which opened from the passage, found some clothing. This I hastily put on, and then went to the door of the room which Karl told me was being used by Fraülein Skoda and Frau Gretchen. Here I knocked; softly at first, and then more loudly, calling to Frau Gretchen to come and speak with me. This, after a short delay, she did, opening the door from the inside and peering out at me. But immediately that she saw my face in the light of the candle which she was holding, she screamed aloud, and running back called in a voice of terror to Fraülein Skoda that it was I.

And she, hastily putting on a long, soft gown came out to me. When she saw me standing in the doorway, there was no sign of fear in her eyes, only I thought a great gladness, as she put her hands into mine, and whispered: "You are not dead, you are not drowned?" The very words, I thought, that Karl had used, but yet how differently they sounded in my ears coming from her lips.

"No, Wilhelmina," I answered, smiling down into her face, which flushed daintily at my using of her name, "but I will tell you about that, and more, at another time. My brother Daubeney and I have come to take you out from here while Count Czvargas is away. Dress quickly," I went on, "and come!" and yet for all the need of haste, I did not wish to loose her hands from mine. But she would not let me wait in the cold, dark passage, but led me into a small room adjoining her bed-chamber, where there was a bright fire burning. There I sat, waiting, while I heard her and Frau Gretchen hurrying to and fro in the next room, making ready for their sudden and surprising journey.

The warmth of the fire, the comfort of my cushioned chair, and the ease of mind at our happier prospects lulled me with a sense of delight, so that the minutes slipped by unheeded. But I had just roused myself and risen to my feet, to urge them to more haste, when I heard footsteps coming down the passage, and going to the door, found Daubeney there. Wilhelmina coming from her chamber at the same moment we all met in the passage-way.

Daubeney greeted the maiden with a grave, tired smile, and turning to me said shortly:—

"Come with me!" jerking his head back, as he spoke, in the direction of the gate. And I, fearing from his look of seriousness that what we most hoped to avoid had come about, asked Fraülein Skoda to remain behind for a few minutes, while I hurriedly followed my brother. He said nothing, but when we reached the gate before which Karl was faithfully standing, he led me to the grille, and drawing back the shutter, pointed out. I looked, and was not surprised at what I saw, though the sight filled me with a strange feeling of rage and dread. Were Daubeney and I, I thought, to be beaten at every turn

by this brigand ruffian, Czvargas?   For as
I looked I saw in the light of the bright moon
(it being now about the hour of midnight)
the Count and his army of mounted men
slowly riding up the causeway.

Yet it was a strange thing to me that from
that moment all my sense of weariness should
leave me, though my body was so weak and
exhausted ; but the need to act and act quickly
(Daubeney, as ever, leaving all to me) brought
my mind back to a state of keenest wakeful-
ness.   First I saw that all the bolts were
shot fairly into their places, and that the
guard-room door was closed upon the two
bound men, who no doubt wondered still
what we were going to do with them.   Then
telling Karl to stand ready with his pistol,
I waited by Daubeney, leaning against the
wall.   My brother and I also had pistols
which we had taken from the two sentinels.

As we waited, hearing the men come slowly
nearer, I thought that some purpose might
be served, but what I knew not, by holding
our peace, so that the knowledge of who
held the Castle might be kept from Count
Czvargas.   At least nothing could be gained

for us by telling him. And even as I thought this I knew that there could now be only one way for us to get away from the Castle, and that by the same way that I had left it. Only that! but now there was no time for further thought, for the great voice of Count Czvargas calling for the opening of the gates sounded through the silent night. And, not waiting for the sentinel's answering cry, "who goes?" he gave the word in a clear voice that, I thought, had also a touch of tenderness in it :—

"Wilhelmina, Wilhelmina, Wilhelmina!" and at the sound I heard a rustle at my side, and a soft hand stole into mine, and looking down I saw her whose name he cried shrinking back from his rude calling of it. But there was no answer to him, only the silence and our beating hearts, while I pressed Wilhelmina's hand in mine. Then a muttered oath came from the Count, and loosing her hand, I whispered to Wilhelmina to go; which she did, reluctantly, as far as the passage-door, standing within the doorway with Frau Gretchen. We then heard the sound of the Count dismounting from his horse, and striding to the gate he thundered at it with his pistol-butt, swearing loudly as he did so.

"Wake up, you lazy, useless hounds!" he shouted, "wake up and open the gate! By G——, but you shall pay dearly for this!" And though the thickness of the high walls deadened his voice and also the closed door of the guard-room, I could fancy that the wretched men within trembled as they lay there bound and helpless. And once more Count Czvargas thundered on the gate and swore. But I smiled to think how, for a time at least, we were in the better position, and that the defence of his strong Castle was being used against him who had planned it so well: and yet there would be little chance of mercy to Daubeney and me, or of ransom, if we fell again into his hands. Thinking to let him know that there was no entrance for him and his this night, I signed to Karl to draw aside the shutter, slowly. As he did this, and only an inch or two of it was open, the Count's sword came driving through the crack to its full length, the hilt striking the iron gate with a sharp clang, its blade lightly grazing my cheek. In my anger I clapped my pistol to the grille and pulled the trigger. And there followed upon my fire a great stamping of a horse's feet and snorting, and an angry cry of pain from a man's voice; and the sword leapt back as quickly as it came.

And then there broke out from the Count so foul a stream of oaths and threats and cursing as I cannot write down here. So vile were they that I was fain to close the door leading to Fraülein Skoda's passage, and I saw that she had placed her hands upon her ears and was returning to her room. When I came again to the gate, taking another pistol and holding it carefully as I looked, I ventured to peer through the grille, and saw that the Count had given the order to retreat, and that, in much confusion of turning and backing horses this was being done, Count Czvargas cursing the men for their slowness and the delay. I saw also that the Count's bridle arm was hurt, for that he held it to his chest while he caught the reins in his right hand and mounted heavily upon his horse. And it gave me a savage pleasure to think that I had hurt this man who had given so much pain to us, and was like enough to give us more ere we were free of him. As he turned to move away, he looked back at the Castle, and I saw that his great black beard was flecked with angry froth, and that his face was dark with hate and rage, as through clenched teeth he hissed out words of threatening which I could not catch.

But now, at least, he and his men were going, for a time, and we could take some rest; and seeing them go, all my strength went suddenly away, and I felt that I should fall. But I was weak with hunger more than with weariness, though scarce twelve hours had passed since I had eaten, and with Daubeney it was the other way. So telling him to lie down and get some rest, and bidding Karl watch the gate meanwhile, keeping the shutter drawn so that he could mark the movements of the Count, I went once more to Fraülein Skoda's room, and asked the good Frau Gretchen to get me some food. This she did at once, regarding me the while with silent awe, Wilhelmina also helping her to place the bread and meat upon the table; and, sitting before the fire, I ate most greedily, and as I ate I fell asleep.

When I awoke and looked round guiltily, wondering where I was, I met Fraülein Skoda's face smiling into mine; and seated by her side, eating valiantly of the food which Frau Gretchen placed before him, was my brother Daubeney. It was near noon, and Daubeney and I had slept while the faithful Karl kept the gate, but he, becoming overcome with want of sleep, and wishing to know what should be done with the two bound men, had wakened Daubeney, who finding me asleep, had waited, by Fraülein Skoda's suggestion, to satisfy some of his huge hunger before he woke me. To my surprise I learnt from him that Count Czvargas had made no further attempt to get within the Castle, only setting a strong guard at the end of the causeway to prevent our escape. Either, I thought, he would wait and starve us into surrender, or more likely, obtain some cannon with which to batter down the gate; but whichever of these he did would give us time.

Hungrily sniffing my brother's steaming

meal, but thinking more of quitting the presence of Wilhelmina, I went out, leaving the two together.   Karl I told to go and get food for our prisoners and himself, while I kept the gate.   I had much to think about. First these two men, what to do with them? To place them in the cell which I had myself occupied was my first thought; but we had none to spare to act as guard of prisoners. The easiest plan would be to let them go, though I did not wish that they should tell Count Czvargas how few we were.   As I paced to and fro, Karl appeared, bringing food for them.   A far more liberal supply, I thought, than Count Czvargas gave to his prisoners.   The men were glad to see the food, and us also, having no doubt been looking for such an end as in like case their master would have sent them to.   As Karl unbound their arms I saw in their faces the same relief that I had felt when my own arms were loosed.   Their names, they told me, were Kaspar and Johann, and Kaspar I knew now as the man whom Count Czvargas stunned with a blow for yawning at his lengthy speech.

" Now, men," I said, as they ate greedily of the food, "eat well, for it is the last meal that you will have in Castle Czvargas." At that they stopped eating and stared up at me. " For," I went on, " when you have eaten, I shall open the gate and let you free." At my words Kaspar looked up beseechingly at me and said that to go out would be certain death. " Rather would I drown," he said, " than give Count Czvargas the chance of killing me with torture!" and he shivered. But Johann said nothing, returning to his food. " Will you serve me, then?" I asked, " and take your chance of escape with us?"

" Yes, that will I!" Kaspar cried eagerly, and Johann also when I asked him for his answer. So I unbound the men, and for a time let Kaspar stand with me, while Johann remained shut within the guard-room, Karl going away to get some needful sleep. During the time of my watch I talked with Kaspar, and heard from him much concerning the Count, but little of any service to me, save that the provisions of the Castle were something low, the expedition upon which the Count had gone having been in the hope of replenishing them. But I did not think it likely that we should be here long enough to feel the want of food, rather did this knowledge help to strengthen my hope that Count Czvargas would be content to wait until he had starved us out.

During my watch Fraülein Skoda came to me once, bringing some food and a cup of wine, which I took gladly, and thinking of that other time in Venice when I drank "Auf Wiedersehen," I looked towards her as I raised the cup to my lips; but she would not meet my look, feigning to be filled with interest in the captive soldier, who himself regarded her and me with strange wonder; so that, feeling rebuffed, I drained the cup alone.

Karl waking at about the hour of six, asked that he might take the night watch, and I, glad to go within, allowed him.

When I entered Fraülein Skoda's room, which we now used in common as a dining-place (my brother and I having chosen as our bed-chamber the room leading from the passage next the gate), I found her seated beside Daubeney, looking eagerly into his face while he recounted his adventures and the evil chances by which he was taken prisoner by Count Czvargas. So I sat down and listened too; but the sight of these two, whom I loved most in the world, talking together easily, and the light in Wilhelmina's eyes, and the little notice that they took of me when I came in—all this gave me a strange feeling of anger and discomfort which I felt then for the first time.

Daubeney was telling of the time when he had left the Castle, and the Count had bid him " Auf Wiedersehen."

"When I reached the road," he said, " I heard, borne on the quiet air, the noise of horsemen issuing from the Castle, and I darted into the bushes at the roadside, being caught in a horrid bog that took me to my knees. So I returned again to the road, running along it as fast as I was able; but finding that this seemed to take me farther from the lake at every step, I again essayed to push my way through the bushes to the shore, getting caught once more in the swamp and losing much time, so that I blamed myself for this delay as I hurried on in the darkness. After a long while, as it seemed to me, I came upon the lake again, and as I reached it, looking up towards the Castle, I saw a light upon the water.   Believing this to be from a boat, I hastened on the road again, but after going some way, I thought it wiser to conceal myself until these men had passed.   Which they did presently, not, as I had thought, upon the water; but having left the boat, they came walking quickly along the road within easy sight of me had they thought to look for me ; and from their talk I perceived that they were following me.   So I waited among the bushes, wondering what I should do, but thinking it best to let the men get well ahead before I followed them or went back towards the shore.   Then I thought of the boat, but when, seeking it, I reached the bank of the lake, I saw it drifting slowly away in the moonlight, and as I thought, empty.   How you received me, Frank, when I swam out to it, you know!"

But Fraülein Skoda did not know, and all my hardness to Daubeney had to be told to her ; at which she only laughed ; which was the strangest thing to me.   And then

I went on to tell her of our scuffle with the soldiers, and of Karl's news that brought us to the Castle.

And so we talked, we three, merry and careless for a time, glad to forget the seriousness of our case, glad to persuade our willing minds that the present hour at least was given us for our enjoyment. Then I urged Daubeney to tell us of his adventures, which thereupon he did.

CHAPTER XII.

DAUBENEY'S STORY.

AFTER leaving Munich Daubeney and the man Bellew reached Gralzburg safely, but Daubeney stayed there for a day to rest the horses and to learn all that he could of the pleasantest roads for his further journey. At Spätz again they were delayed by the lameness of Bellew's horse, and Daubeney, not wishing to be longer on the way than he could help, went by himself to a neighbouring village for the purpose of purchasing another in its stead, arranging with Bellew to meet him on foot at a place about five miles from Spätz, from where he intended that they should travel that same day as far as Berlau. The little village of Breczin was in *fête*, the place being thronged with country people, with here and there a brigand-looking soldier who by his noisy, rollicking manner strove to impress the peasants with an idea of his importance.

Daubeney's size and his uncommon dress attracted more attention than he liked, but except for a bold remark from one of the soldiers, some of whom tried to engage him in conversation, he was unmolested. He bought a good horse, and while paying for it, some one jostled his elbow, with intent as he believed, causing him to spill a number of gold pieces from his pouch. The sight of the money must have excited the greed of the man who was the occasion of the accident, for as Daubeney moved away, leading the new horse, he saw that he was being followed by some of the brigands. He took no notice of them, however, but reaching the inn, which he had chosen by reason of its remoteness from the crowded part of the village, put the horse with his own, and entered the house for his dinner. He could not eat in private, as he would have wished, there being only one common-room. While he was eating, two or three of the brigands entered the room, and after looking at him, left again without taking anything to eat or drink. Then two of them, larger than the others, came in, and finding seats near Daubeney, called for drink, and began in a loud voice to remark on my brother's foreign looks. As he went on eating, however, without noticing their remarks, they addressed him openly in a bullying tone, jeering at him, and trying, as Daubeney thought, to engage him in a quarrel. But he was too wise to let himself get mixed up in a brawl with such ruffianly-looking fellows (his temper being less easily roused than mine), the more particularly as it seemed to him that the host of the inn was aware of the intentions of the men, and was encouraging them.

Finishing his meal, therefore, as quickly as he could, and without giving a glance at these noisy scoundrels, he paid his reckoning, and mounting his own horse and leading the other, pushed his way as quickly as he might through the crowded, narrow street in the direction of the road leading back to Spätz, towards the place where he had arranged to meet Bellew.

He rode as quickly as he was able, encumbered by the led horse, hoping that by his air of indifference he might have persuaded the brigands to let him be. And as he was beginning to feel more secure, he suddenly became aware that he was being followed, and looking back he saw three ruffians galloping after him. He urged on the horses, but found that the others were gaining on him at every stride. Seeing that he could not avoid being overtaken, he pulled up and dismounting quickly tied the new horse to a tree, mounted his own again, and turned to face his pursuers. The men checked their horses for a minute when they saw the stand he made, but after a short talk among themselves they once more made for him together. And Daubeney, resolving to die hard, levelled his pistol at the nearest man and fired when only a distance of ten paces remained between them. But a movement of his own horse and the sudden check which the robber gave to his caused the aim to be wild, so that the horse received the bullet intended for his master. The horse stumbled and fell headlong, taking the rider with him to the ground. Meanwhile the other two had rushed on at Daubeney together, and at one of them Daubeney struck savagely with his sword, without effect by reason of the restlessness of his horse which was frightened by the unaccustomed sight; but Daubeney himself received a blow upon the head which struck him from his horse and stunned him.

Not waiting to learn if he were alive or dead, the ruffians rifled his pockets of all that they contained, and he whose horse was wounded taking Daubeney's and the other he had newly bought, rode off with their booty, leaving Daubeney lying in the road. At this time the roads were empty, all who were going to the *fête* having passed along, and none thinking of returning so early in the day. When Daubeney came again to his senses, he found Bellew leaning over him, he having reached the place appointed just in time to see the robbers galloping away.

But for a sharp, throbbing pain in his head, Daubeney was uninjured, and so the two returned to Spätz on foot, reaching the inn late in the evening, weary and travel-stained. By great good fortune the thieves had been content with taking Daubeney's money, all that he had for the journey to Venice, but had not taken the papers which he carried in a wallet next to his skin. One of these papers was a note of credit on our uncle's house which he had given to Daubeney lest his money should run out. By means of this Daubeney was able to obtain a further supply of money from a merchant in Spätz.

But on the day following the thieves' attack upon him, when he tried to get from his bed, my brother found that he could not stand for the dizziness which beset him, and Bellew becoming frightened by the wandering of his talk, brought a surgeon to him. He, by frequent bleedings, reduced the fever in his blood, but also weakened him so much, that he was forced to remain in Spätz for the space of four weeks. And when at length they started on their journey, Daubeney was able to travel for only a short distance on each day.

The host of the Spätz inn gave them the fullest news of roads and inns, of which Daubeney was most glad, for more than once he would have been tempted, by reason of his weariness, to rest at other places than those spoken of by this man. And thus it happened on one day, when, having travelled fifteen miles by very bad roads and in pouring rain,

they came to a wayside house ; and Daubeney,
trusting to chance to befriend him, determined
to stay here, rather than plod on for another
weary, wet five miles to the inn which they
had hoped to reach before nightfall.   The
place had little to recommend it in appearance ;
and it was long before Daubeney could get
any answer to the summons which he thundered on the rickety door.   When his patience
was almost exhausted, and, despite the rain
which was falling in torrents, he had nearly
decided on pushing on to the next house,
he heard sounds of some one moving within ;
and presently the door was opened by a sour-
faced woman, who after regarding the two
men keenly for a moment, banged the door
to in their faces, but not before Daubeney
had placed his foot in the opening to prevent
it from shutting.   At this the woman sent out
such a screech of wicked oaths at him, that
drawing away his foot, he let her close the
door, feeling, as he heard her shooting the
bolts, that to seek shelter there was hopeless.

It was now gathering dusk, and the two
weary travellers were not wishful to spend
the night in the open air and the cold rain,

so they went round to the stables, thinking to get shelter there until the force of the storm was spent, or till daylight came again to show them on their difficult way.

Picking their steps carefully through a mass of filth and mud they reached an outhouse at the back, where they were able to put their horses and to shelter themselves. More, they found some fodder, which they were glad enough to give to the tired animals, wishing at the same time that there might also have been some food for themselves. As they had led their horses across the yard, another horse had whinnied, and Daubeney, wondering what kind of beast this strange woman would keep, went to look at it, finding a strong, well-kept animal in a good stable.

After a time, the rain abating a little, Daubeney determined to try again if he could not obtain some food and warmth inside the house. Going to the back, and opening a door which he found on the latch, he came into the kitchen, before the fire of which the woman was engaged in cooking. She seemed not to notice my brother's coming, and concluding that she was deaf, he went near and touched her shoulder. At that she darted away from him, sending a look of such malignant fury at my brother that he was for a moment taken aback. But thinking it useless to try to speak to her, he drew a gold piece from his pouch, and pointing from it to the meat which frizzled on the fire, and from thence to his mouth, showed the woman that he wished to pay for his supper. And indeed the pleasant smell of the meat was causing a copious moisture in his hungry mouth. The eyes of the hag glistened at sight of the gold, and pointing to Bellew, who had followed Daubeney into the house, she held up two fingers, grinning greedily; and Daubeney nodded, glad to get food and shelter even at so high a price, not thinking that there could be any danger in displaying his wealth so carelessly to this wretched woman.

She now bustled about actively enough, and before long placed a meal before them to which they were most glad to help themselves. While they were eating, the woman, casting sharp, curious glances at them, passed back and forwards from the fire to the door, peering out keenly as though looking for some one. And presently, after Daubeney and Bellew had washed down their meal with a bottle of sour wine which the woman, with many signs of the honour she was doing them by allowing them to drink, produced from a cupboard, they heard the sound of a horseman splashing along the road at a hand-gallop, showing that he at least knew the way well.

The woman, too, was aware of the man's coming, for she hurried out to meet him, closing the door carefully behind her. Daubeney, wishing to learn what she might be at, rose and attempted to follow her, finding, to his annoyance, that the door was bolted on the outside. Moreover, the fumes of the wine, which was stronger than he had thought, and of which he had drunk freely by reason of his thirst, had mounted to his head, which after his late illness was like to have been less able to stand the strength of the raw spirit with which the wine had doubtless been mixed. He leapt out into the yard from the window, however, falling on the slippery stones as he did so. Bellew followed him, and together they crossed to where they saw a lantern burning. The noise of their steps was deadened by the swish of the wind and the stamping of the man's horse, from which he was taking the saddle. Concealing themselves behind a door that flapped noisily in the wind, they tried to learn from the talk of the woman and her son—for such he appeared to be—something of the kind of place that they had come to. And this would have been easy enough had Daubeney been able to understand the jargon in which they spoke; for the man shouted his words into the woman's ear so that they could be heard above the storm. But they spoke in so outlandish a dialect, that Daubeney was able to make little sense of what they said. Only that the woman seemed to be urging her son to some action which he was not wishful to perform. But she gained her wish in the end; for the man, going to the stable, brought out the horse which Daubeney had lately admired, and proceeded to get him ready for a journey.

Thinking that he had learnt enough, my brother drew Bellew back with him to the house, and entering by the same window, sat before the fire. Soon after, the woman came in also, and by signs, showed them that she would take them to their bedchamber. Nor was Daubeney sorry to go there, for a great sleepiness had taken hold of him. But his anxiousness was not lessened when he heard the woman bolting their door (which me-thought was a habit of the women in these parts). But his mind was made so stupid and drowsy by the full meal and the bad wine, that he lay down, dressed, and soon fell asleep, hearing as he closed his eyes, the sound of a horseman galloping away.

When he awoke, after three or four hours, with a thickness of his head which was most unpleasant, he roused Bellew, and fearing to remain in what seemed to them a thieves' den, they got out by the window, and securing their horses, went slowly on their way.

After losing the road once, and getting back in the early light of the morning nearly to the same place again, they at length reached the house of Frau Gretchen, where Daubeney had been advised to stay by the host of the Spätz inn. Here they gladly stopped, resting for the whole of that day and the next night.

When they left the inn on the following

morning, Daubeney's mind was oppressed by a strange sense of coming evil, and after trying to shake it off, he told Bellew of it, ashamed of himself in the telling. But Bellew was quite ready to believe anything which had about it a savour of witchery, and had his own stories to tell his master of others whom he knew, to whom death or dreadful accident had followed after such fears as Daubeney now felt. This did not add to my brother's cheerfulness, so that he felt as he never had before, that some evil would befal him, and soon.

Now though I have myself had fears of the same kind a score of times, yet can I not remember one that was fulfilled; so I believe that with Daubeney it was caused by his late illness, and the natural dread following upon the events of the night in the bad inn, looking as he did for some sign of being followed by such robbers as had beset him once before.

And yet I can but say that had it not been for this consuming dread that oppressed him at this time, I should never have learnt any-thing of what happened to him after, nor would my uncle have come into the happy possession of his papers. For so strong was this feeling upon my brother, that he began to tell Bellew all that he should do if he himself were killed, and into his care he gave those papers of which I have already spoken, telling him to place them securely under his clothing, and to defend them with all care. Little thinking that the faithful servant Bellew was so soon to come by a cruel death.

And strange though it yet seems to me, Bellew had scarcely bestowed the precious wallet next his skin, when they heard the sound of horses coming up behind them, and looking back they saw mounted soldiers to the number of ten or twelve. They were unable to conceal themselves, the country here being open, so they drove spurs into their horses, and galloped off as fast as they were able. But the soldiers' horses were fleeter and lighter than theirs, which had been chosen for strength in taking a long journey more than for riding in a race; and seeing that the brigands gained upon them rapidly, Daubeney called to Bellew to stop, and together they turned and faced the band of ruffians that came thundering on, swooping down upon them, brandishing their swords, and uttering outlandish cries. Daubeney, expecting to die, determined to sell his life dearly. But Bellew fell dead before his eyes with a pistol shot through his breast and a great slashing cut from a man's sword. Yet Daubeney was not shot, nor, to his amazement, even struck at; but immediately that Bellew had fallen the men drew back, and one who seemed to be in command called upon Daubeney to surrender. My brother's answer was to set spurs to his horse and to charge headlong at the brigands, flinging his pistol which had missed fire into the midst of them. For some moments he kept them at bay, striking out valiantly with his giant's strength, as I can well believe, and sorely wounding two of the men; but his horse being shot under him, he fell to the ground, and before he could regain his feet, was fallen upon by four of the ruffians, who, after a great struggle, succeeded in securing him. He was then taken to that same inn where Bellew and he had spent so ill a night, and from there, on the following morning, bound and most carefully guarded to Castle Czvargas.

Among his captors he saw the man who had seemed to be the son of the woman of the inn, and through whose news of him to Count Czvargas my brother doubtless owed his being taken prisoner. I also knew something of this man, for he was no other than that same Fritz by whose hands I had been cast into the lake. After arriving at the Castle, Daubeney became ill of a fever, which was upon him for many days; but as this left him, he was surprised (as in my own case I had been) at the care which was taken of him. Once he was summoned into the presence of Count Czvargas, who had discoursed to him of the pleasure of the life led by him and his men, asking Daubeney openly to join his band. On other occasions, too, the Count had shown my brother a rough kindness which he was unable to understand, and which was due, I think, to his great size and strength, and the Count's desire to win him over, and also to a certain charm in Daubeney which all who meet him feel. Of

the ransom which was expected Daubeney
knew nothing, nor of my coming to the
Castle, nor of Fraülein Skoda's presence there,
until he saw us on that day of the show of
wrestling of which I have already told you.

CHAPTER XIII.

HOW I LEFT CASTLE CZVARGAS, AND HOW FRITZ SAW A GHOST.

THEN I told my story, much as I have put it here, but more briefly, and with little mention of Fraülein Skoda, save of my meeting with her at Venice and in the forest (though Daubeney had not spoken of his meeting her at all); and by the time that we had finished it was very late, so, bidding Fraülein Skoda good-night, Daubeney and I went to our room. I, pleading great weariness, asked my brother to relieve Karl during the night, so that I might have a good night's rest. To this Daubeney agreed readily and without surprise or question, as was always his unselfish way, though I had not yet told him of my reason for wishing it.

It was this. I believed that the sooner we were away from the Castle, the less likely would it be that Count Czvargas would suspect that it had been possible for us to leave it without his knowledge, trusting, as I hoped, to keep us (whoever we were) locked in until such time as our provisions were exhausted, to which end he had placed the guard at the farther end of the causeway, where we could see the watch fires brightly burning.   But I had no thought to get out by that way, but rather by the old way from the Castle to the lake, and with the help of the boat in which Daubeney and I had already saved ourselves once.   I was meaning, therefore, on the next night, to swim to the boat and to bring it back, if indeed I found it and were able to row it so far.   Even if I failed, as I hoped not to do, the case of those who remained would be no worse than it was now. That I might be the better prepared for this hard task which I wished to perform, it was needful that I should get all the rest I could this night, and so I had, as I have said, asked Daubeney to watch while I slept.

Though the thought of the long, cold swim which was before me, with its hopes and dangers, might have occupied my mind, it was not that which kept me awake when I lay down to sleep. It was not that, but something which, it seemed, concerned but me alone when I should be thinking only of the common good. And yet you will not wonder at it, you who read, for Wilhelmina, as I thought, was mine by right; I had loved her first, though Daubeney had seen her before ever I knew her name or that she lived. And now he, too, loved her, as I believed and could not wonder at, for who could help it? Many others whom I had never seen might love her too, and surely did, else were they blind—with them I was ready to take my chance. But Daubeney, my brother, him I could not fight against, even in the matter of my lady's love. Only wait, and long, and let her choose. And she? I have come last to this. While Daubeney was speaking of his travels and exploits, modestly and quietly, as was his wont, but with an ease and elegance of speech that I have not, Wilhelmina regarded him eagerly with her great admiring eyes, while I jealously watched the gleam that came into them as she followed the recounting of his story; and more than all, I noted the sigh which came from her when Daubeney's tale was done. But while I told mine, she looked into the fire, thoughtfully and yet carelessly as it seemed to me, and once only had I been able, though all the time I tried, to make her look into my eyes, and then but for a moment, her eyelids fluttering and dropping over the eyes which I so wished to look into mine; and that was when I had come in my story to where I met with her in the forest, and she had looked quickly up at me, to keep me, as I thought, from telling Daubeney of her being dressed in a boy's clothes, and weeping as though her heart would break. It made my own heart ache now to think of it, that and the heedless manner of her listening to me, who once, I had thought, regarded me with a more than common interest.

Yet I could not wonder at it. For who would look twice at me with Daubeney by? His great giant's body and kind, gentle face were surely made for a woman's regard, and his quiet disposition for her love. Yet I could love too, I thought, as deeply and more fiercely than he, despite my smaller frame and plainer face.

So that, such thoughts as these driving through my restless mind, I did not get so much sleep that night as I wished for, and at about the hour of six I rose, and going to the gate, sent Daubeney to bed, he having been on guard since three. But at about eight o'clock, so great a sleepiness beset me, my eyes shutting for all my striving to keep them open, that I sent Kaspar to wake Karl; and he, coming to my relief, I lay down again and slept soundly until noon, waking to find my body and my mind much rested.

No message had come yet from Count Czvargas, nor threat, nor sign of action. Only the sight of the men patiently guarding the causeway, cutting off our retreat; so that we concluded that the Count knew, as none should better, how useless it would be to try to force an entrance into his strong Castle without the aid of cannon.

During the rest of the day I went round the Castle, examining with special care the apartments of the Count. Here I found, still hanging by a nail from the wall, Daubeney's Belt and mine. These I gladly took, and my brother and I wore them thereafter.

But as I came again into the room where we took our meals, expecting to find Daubeney there, the delight I felt at getting my Belt again and the thought of Daubeney's pleasure at seeing his, were driven from my mind by the sight that met my jealous eyes. For through the window looking upon the court-yard I saw Daubeney walking, and Fraülein Skoda by his side, looking up into his face as he spoke to her. As I saw them, the maiden turned and caught my look, and blushed red at my seeing her thus. Frau Gretchen coming into the room and seeing me turning away from regarding them, looked at me, grinning foolishly, so that I could have struck her, and said :—

" Little maidens ever love great men ! "

And I strode angrily away, not wishing that the woman should see how much her thoughtless words pained me, revealing as they did, that even she had noticed Fraülein Skoda's better liking of my brother. Yet was not Wilhelmina so little, rather did she look small only beside my giant brother, her comely head, as I knew well, reaching above my own shoulder.

But when the sun was getting low, I ate a great meal, for that I knew not when next I might get one, and telling Karl to be ready with a strong rope at the opening of the Castle wall (Daubeney being on guard), I told Fraülein Skoda of my project. And it was strange to me (and indeed for long after I still thought it strange, not yet having come to a better understanding of the ways of women) that when I spoke of the swim which I was about to take, she threw out both her hands to mine, and so deep a light flashed from her eyes that I marvelled at it. But she said nothing; only that her blue eyes slowly welled up with tears, as, loosing my hands from their sweet imprisonment, she turned away and looked through the window upon the bare courtyard. And I had no words to say, only thoughts of wonder at her excellent beauty and my love for her; and even as I looked I thought that it had been strange indeed if Daubeney had not loved her too. So I said "Good-bye,"—just that, and going slowly to the door, went out. But as I crossed the threshold, I heard her steps behind me and the rustle of her dress, and felt her hand upon my arm, as in a broken voice, whispering, she cried :—

"God send you come back safe to—to us!" and she turned again to the window, while I, wishing that her last word had been "me," and hardly able to see for the great pain of parting from her that filled my eyes, stumbled across the courtyard, catching a glimpse of her standing at the closed window, waving a kerchief to me. And as I grasped the rope which Karl had tied to a stout post that had doubtless been used before for a like purpose, I closed my eyes that this might be my last sight of the Castle Czvargas, if it so happened that I should not return to it.

For the venture upon which I was engaging was greater than any other that I had done, though it may seem a slight thing for a man to do—to swim six miles and bring a boat back. And so it might have been, but for the coldness of the water and the strangeness of the lake currents, and the need to go so quietly for the fear of being heard or seen, and, more than all, the doubt whether the boat would still be where Daubeney and I had left it ; with the prospect for me, then, of having to swim back against the cold lake-currents with the chance of being taken or ever I got back. Of hunger I did not think, for it is hard to know how great the hunger of a man may be when at the time of starting he is full and satisfied. But before I returned to the Castle Czvargas I was hungry indeed, and aching with deep weariness.

But now I saw only Wilhelmina's sad face and her waving kerchief as my feet touched the water and I stood upon the slab of rock.

Here I took off all my clothing, and tying it with the rope bade Karl draw it up to him. I could take no other weapon than a knife, which, fixed in the belt that I wore about my waist, was all I had with me. Then, with a fervent prayer, which came unknowing to my lips, I let myself quietly into the water and began to swim.

The sky was overcast, with a sharp wind from the mountains that blew keenly in my face, and I could see no stars, so that I trusted to the feel of the current to take me where I wished to go. But presently a great rush of biting wind came, with driving rain that stung me with its sharp coldness, lashing my face like hail. For a long time, as it seemed to me, this squall raged, and I had almost thought that I should need to return to the Castle, for that the wind and rain drove me back more than my swimming took me on, when the storm as suddenly died away, and a thin, straight rain fell. But the surface of the water was ruffled much, so that there was no longer need to swim with the same quietness and stealth, though by this there was not much fear of being seen by reason of my distance from the shore and the deep darkness of the water. And so I swam on, wondering how far I had come, and wishing much that I might catch, were it only for a moment, a glimpse of the shore. This want of knowledge of how far I had travelled and had yet to travel was more disquieting to me than any other thing, so that before I had swam four miles I was overcome with weariness and with the great dread of failing in my task.

But I called to mind, with comfort, a saying of my father's, that "an Englishman should always be able to go on for ten more minutes"; which before had seemed to me a strange and boastful saying, in that it would seem to mean for ever, since one ten minutes past another would but begin. And yet, I say, it was a great comfort to me, and a help such as I had not thought possible—that I, an English boy, as Count Czvargas in his contempt had called me, had set myself this task to do, and could yet go on for so much longer in my struggle to succeed in it. "Ten minutes more!" I repeated constantly to myself, until my senses were dulled with the repeating of the words, and they came to lose all meaning. "Ten minutes more, an Englishman can always go," I muttered. "Ten minutes more, Wilhelmina!" for my mind, which had been dwelling upon her and the hope of saving her and Daubeney, began, I think, to wander, and my numbed limbs ached and moved stiffly almost without my knowledge, so that I drifted more than I swam. Then, the sky becoming clearer, I saw that the moon was rising above the mountains, and, as in a dream, I knew that I must do my utmost now to get on before it became too light.

As I thought this, and made a weak last

effort to force my body through the water, I found that I was being taken along more quickly in the direction of my right hand, and also that the water went suddenly even colder than before. So I turned slowly over on to my back, and paddling with my hands, let the current take me where it would ; and looking round in a few moments, my mind something clearer by this short rest and the glad knowledge that I learnt, I saw that I was at that spot where Daubeney and I had gone ashore before our struggle with the three men ; and my spirits rose as I let the stream take me slowly along the bank and safely past the point where the road came on to the lake, and so down towards the opening to the river. Then I turned over again, and with feeble, fitful strokes urged my body on for the last half-mile. "Ten minutes more!" I cried, as my teeth chattered in my head. Slowly, wearily I made my way on, until, at last, under the bright light of the risen moon, I saw the boat. So glad a sight I had seldom seen! it was not gone! Hope came back to me with a great surging wave of joy, and striking out with all my remaining strength (which was but little), I clutched the boat, and stiffly and with great pain clambered into it, and flinging myself down, lay there for the space of some minutes, breathing hard and with closed eyes.

But the cold was so sharp that I knew I must not stay as I was, so I groped my way to where, when I left it in such haste, I had thrown the grey cloak which had before been so warm a comfort to me. Taking this in my hands, I stood up to wrap it well round my frozen body. It was a foolish thing to do, to stand upright in the clear light of the moon, but I had no thought of being seen here in the lonely silence of the stream; and indeed my mind was too numbed to think of anything but how best to warm it and my body into some feeling of life again.

As I stood thus, with my arms above my head, holding the good cloak behind me, my eyes went to the bank, and opened wide with fear at the sight that met them there. Crouched behind a bush so that one half of his body was in view, holding a pistol pointed at my head, was the soldier Fritz! I knew him at once, though I was standing with my face full towards the moon. For a moment we remained so, neither of us moving; I, frozen into a helpless stillness by the horror of a certain death, the dulness of my mind keeping me from acting to prevent that which I stupidly knew must come, wondering numbly why he did not fire, wishing even that he would; and so little things burn into a man's mind at such moments. I remember that I noticed on his left cheek, where the moonlight caught it, an odd scar made by two deep lines which met so as to form a letter V, and wondered how the man had come by them; but still he did not fire as I stood waiting for my death, my arms above my head, holding the cloak, my body shimmering in the bright moonlight, the drops of water glistening as they trickled down my limbs, the gentle rocking of the boat causing me to sway to and fro, the faint, cold breeze fluttering the cloak behind me. All in a moment, before I had taken one breath; and as I looked, a great shock of horror leaped into the man's startled eyes, and his jaw dropped. And it came to me, so suddenly that I uttered a gasping cry more like a moan than any other

sound, that this man, who himself had cast me
into the Lake Czvargas, now regarded me as
a spirit of the lake come here to haunt him
for his cruel crime. At the moment of my
thought, his hand fell to his side, loosing the
pistol, and dropping on his knees, his eyes
still fixed upon mine with a look of terror, he
made on his breast the holy sign of the Cross.
And I, hardly knowing that I did it, stepped
towards him ; and as I moved he fell with his
face upon the ground before me, helpless,
ready, as I thought, for the sacrifice. And,
God forgive me! I knew that I must take his
life. I shudder even now to think of it, and
always when at night I wake and lie awake
this one scene comes to me, I and Fritz.
With one quick step I reached the bank, the
cloak dropping from my arms into the boat,
and with another I was at his side, grasping
the knife with my trembling hand. Either
he or I, I thought, trying, how feebly God only
knows, to show my horror-stricken mind that
this was not an act of murder. He or I and
Daubeney and Wilhelmina and Karl, he or
those I loved so much, he or I ! For one
moment I hesitated ; then clenching my teeth,

my breath hissing between them at the sight
of him kneeling there in the helplessness of
his torment, I closed my eyes, and with a
muttered cry for forgiveness, raised my arm
to strike.   But, I thank God for it more than
for all that ever came of joy to me, before my
eyes closed I saw the pistol which the man
had dropped upon the ground ; and in a
moment, a moment of such glad joy of deep
relief that I almost cried out with the pain of
it, I knew that I could do without this crime
of murder.   Dropping the knife, I caught up
the pistol in my hand, and holding it so that
it touched his shoulder called to him to rise.
I doubt not that my voice sounded strange to
him, as it did to me, with a catch of relief in
it and of dread at the thought of what I had
so almost done—what in my heart I had
already done indeed ; but he rose slowly,
turning his wet white face to me.   I pointed
to the boat, and he slowly stepped into it, I
following with the pistol pointed at his face.
Here I made him sit down in the front part
of the boat, and wrapping the cloak quickly
about me, sat facing him, the pistol ready in
my hand.   All in silence, a strange, weird

silence as of the dead. And that he still
thought me to be a spirit I could see from the
way in which he regarded me, keeping his
eyes constantly upon mine in mute terror, and
ever and anon devoutly crossing himself.

CHAPTER XIV.

OF OUR LAST DAYS IN THE CASTLE CZVARGAS.

THEN began, I think, the weariest vigil that man ever kept. I had thought to get some sleep while waiting in the boat until, on the next night, it would be safe for me to row back to the Castle. But now I must needs keep awake to watch this man, for did I close my eyes for a moment, I knew that he would do to me as I had all but done to him ; but though my body cried with pain for rest, and my limbs ached, yet was my mind now wide awake, for a time at least.

So we sat, as far apart as the boat's length would let us, for all that night, until the sun coming up, showed us each other, pale and weary, watching with unsleeping eyes. And not one word had passed between us all the time. Had it not been so cold I think I must have yielded to the great fatigue that held me, but the cold kept me miserably awake, shivering as I sat, one hand holding the pistol, the other grasping tight the cloak about me. And so, through the long day that followed, almost without stirring through all the time we sat, only now and then moving a little to ease our stiff and aching bodies. There was little fear of being seen, for the boat was among the bushes which came down to the stream's bank, unless Count Czvargas should send another after Fritz, if indeed Fritz had been sent by him, and had not come himself to seek for something that might bring reward for him in the finding— that I could not know; nor at this time did I trouble to think; only how I might keep awake and watch this man was all my thought. As the day wore slowly on, hunger came to add to the discomfort of my case, a keen biting hunger with the knowledge added that until I reached the Castle again there would be no hope of staying it.

Not until after midday was the silence between us broken, and then by the man Fritz, who gruffly asked if he might take some sleep, wondering, I doubt not, how much longer I should hold him there, and for what purpose. I nodded to him only, thinking that the sound of my natural voice might take away what fear he still felt, wishing so far as I could to keep over him the influence that rendered him in dread of me. So he lay down, sprawling along the bottom of the boat, and was soon snoring loudly as he slept, while I envied him the comfort of the rest which was denied to me. Yet, the need for watching him so closely being less, I dozed too, my chin falling to my breast while my heavy eyelids drooped ; but only for a few moments at a time, for I would wake with a great sweating start of fear to clutch the pistol, dreading that Fritz waking should find me asleep, and have me at his mercy.

Once, indeed, when I woke thus, it was to see him slowly sitting up, with one hand creeping out towards the pistol in my hand ; but as my eyes came upon him, he fell back again so quickly and so silently that I was in doubt if it had been a dream or no. After that I roused myself, and that I might not fall asleep again I let the cold wind play about my naked body, throwing back the cloak to let it; for the day was dull with a drizzling rain and a sharp wind blowing from the cold mountains. It was torture to me, but better that, I thought, than to be shot dead while sleeping.

As soon as the sun had set behind the forest and it became quite dark, I roused the man, and told him to unfasten the boat from the bank, and then to take the oars and row the boat for me. This he did in a sullen silence, the look of dread passing from his face, and the old cruel look of hate, which I knew better in him, coming in its place. But he rowed well and strongly, so that I was glad that I had him to take me back, for, as I have said, I had no skill in rowing, and doubt that the long journey to the Castle, against the current, and with my back ever towards the point which I was wishing to reach, and also to the enemy who I should have thought ever on the look out for me— all this would have been too great a task for me, even had I slept as I had thought to do during the day. But now I sat facing the Castle, and though I could not see it for the darkness, yet did it seem to come nearer with every powerful stroke of Fritz's arms. The way was longer than my journey down (though to me it was easier), for that we had to keep to the eastern bank of the lake, for fear of being seen by the Count's men, and that there were many curvings and projections of the bank, with swirling contrary currents. But at last I could see the Castle looming out black in the darkness of the night, and felt most cheered by the sight of it, as I had once before. Now, at last, it seemed that there would be some chance for me of sleep and rest, and, after that, of getting out from its imprisoning walls and from the long fell clutches of Count Czvargas.

The moon was not yet up, though the sky was clearer, with a few stars, as I directed Fritz to row to the place where I had entered the water, and, reaching it, to tie the boat to the ring which was driven here into the rock. The rope by which I had come down was hanging there still, so I told Fritz to climb up by it, and to cry the pass word "Somerset." I watched him as he silently obeyed me, and as he went, the great weight of sleepiness and hunger came upon me with a great rush, so that I felt strangely faint, and nearly yielded to the great desire of my eyes to close their heavy lids.

But I roused myself with a last effort, and when Fritz had reached the level of the rock, I stepped from the boat and stood upon the ledge, holding the rope, and waiting for some signal from above for me to follow. I heard him give the word " Somerset," and then he disappeared. And I tightened my hold of the rope, and began to climb up hand over hand; but when I had gone only a few feet, I felt the rope being shaken violently, and not knowing whether this might be a signal for me to hurry on or to go back, I slid quickly down again, my hands burning with the quickness of my descent. And I was scarce in time; for as I reached the ledge of rock and stood upon it, the rope came falling down upon me, leaving me wondering how it had got loose. But I had little time for wonder, for as I looked up in my surprise, I saw a dark form come rushing down towards me. I straightened myself up, pressing against the rock as closely as I was able, and the body of a man fell headlong past me, hitting me so that I fell sprawling into the boat, hurting my side most cruelly against the sharp bows of it. The man's head struck the boat with a loud crack, and without a sound from him, the body sank below the water. In a few moments it appeared again, some two yards off, and sank silently again. I hesitated, not knowing what to think of it, pressing my hand to my side and peering into the darkness of the water to see who it might be, and catching a glimpse of the face as the head rose again, I saw that it was Fritz, dead, as I judged, from the shock of the fall and the blow of his head against the boat; and the surface of the water near him was darkened with blood. Wondering at the strange chance which had brought about his death at the same spot and in something of the same way that he had wished for mine, I looked up again, and saw a face looking down at me, and asked in a whisper who it might be.

"I, Karl," came back the answer, "wait, sir, and I will get another rope." So I waited, as patiently as I might until I saw another rope come dangling down to me. This I grasped, and testing my weight upon it first, slowly, with terrible pain from my side, I climbed to the top, glad to be once more within the Castle. Karl met me as I scrambled up, helping me with his strong arms, but for some moments I lay where I was, closing my eyes tight, and my lips, to keep me from groaning at the great pain of my side, a cutting cough that tinged my lips with blood racking me. As my breath became something easier, I inquired of Karl if all were well, and hearing from him that everything was as when I left the day before, I asked him the reason of Fritz's death, dressing myself as quickly as I could while he told me, and over my clothes wrapping the cloak for greater warmth.

"He gave the word," said Karl, "and thinking it could only be you, Herr Frank, I stood by the post with my hand on the rope; but he, reaching the top, sprang suddenly at me, driving me to the ground, and picking up my knife, which had dropped from my hand as I fell, he hacked at the rope with it, and as I rose, made a plunge at me. But I leaped aside, and clutching his arm, struggled with him; and wrenched the knife from him and drove it into his breast, and as I struck him, he fell backwards over the edge, and I heard his head strike the boat. But he was dead before he fell," he added calmly, as he wiped the knife upon the rope, "and no one will miss him; his comrades hated him for his cruelty, and for that he spied upon them for Count Czvargas." But I thought of his mother, and wondered if she would not mourn her son's death.

Then I told Karl in a few words how I had come upon Fritz, and learning that Daubeney kept the gate, I hastened there to tell him of my success and safety. As I hurried across the courtyard, the great weariness of my body and a hunger which gnawed at my vitals most sorely beset me again, so that, with my hand to my side (which pricked me with a sharp pain as I breathed), I scarce knew where I was going. But when I reached the gate I was astonished at what I saw, and filled with a sudden jealous anger which I was the less able to stay by reason of the weakness and pain of my body. Across the closed doorway of the guard-room my brother lay fast asleep; and I blamed him bitterly for his want of welcome to me, though at any other time I should have known that only the greatest fatigue would have allowed him to go to sleep; and doubtless he had watched all day and into the night to give Karl a good rest, or to let him be on the look out for me at the opening to the lake. But I had no thought of this then, only eyes for his huge sleeping body, and for that other, who, walking to and fro in the faint light of the stars, took Daubeney's place on guard—she, Fraülein Skoda, with a pistol in her hand.

Hearing me approach, she turned quickly to meet me, a smile coming to her face at sight of me, and a crimson blush of shame, as I thought, at being found by me watching in my brother's place, and keeping guard over his sleeping body. And the bitterness of my feeling at Daubeney's easy gain of what I would have striven for with all my power, and of Fraülein Skoda's liking for him, and the vexation of my tired mind and aching body, overcame me, so that I went up to her, and placing my hand upon hers that held the pistol, cried roughly :—

"For shame! Fraülein Skoda ; go to your

room, I pray you, and let a man do this man's work!"   And her face gleamed with a sudden passion that I had never before seen in it, the smile of welcome going from her face like a breath, as she stamped her foot, and answered me, plucking her hand from mine.

"Shame?" she cried, "shame? am I to do nothing, then, Master Frank?   Because I am a girl, can I not take my share, without ——"

And I, ashamed of my weak, jealous anger, but sullen still, broke into her speech, glancing at Daubeney who slept soundly on.

"Pardon! Fraülein Skoda," I said, "I did not think.   I would not wish to hinder you from your desire to help my brother in his watch."   And I turned on my heel, but not so soon as to keep me from hearing her cry in anger and resentment.

"Your brother!" and that was all.   But glancing back, I saw a gleam of anger upon her face that brought bitter tears to her eyes. And as I went on my stubborn way, I muttered to myself :—

"Tum regia Juno acta furore gravi," and it was strange, I thought, that at such a time the only line of Latin that I believe I knew should come uppermost in my mind. So I went away, in my coward's passion, leaving the maiden to her lonely pacing to and fro. Groaning with pain, I fell upon my bed, cursing my evil nature, wondering stupidly why I should love her now more than ever I had before, despite my currish treatment of her. Yet, could this be, I thought, the same timid maiden whose hand had stolen into mine at the time of the Count's coming to the gate, when he had rudely called her name? But even thoughts of her could not keep me long awake, and before I knew it I was fast asleep.

I woke, many hours after, with a feeling of great unhappiness and discomfort, and a sharp pain when I moved, but for some moments could not bring my mind to an understanding of my condition. Then the remembrance of my anger and my boorish rudeness to Fraülein Skoda came to me, bringing a great blush of shame to my cheeks, and I rose hastily, thinking to go and try undo the wrong that I had done. As I rose I found that I could scarce stand, by reason of my hunger and stiffness and sore side, but I went slowly to the room where we took our food, and found there a meal waiting for me, but only Frau Gretchen to welcome me to it, the maiden, as she said, being asleep in her own room; so that the pardon I had thought to ask of Wilhelmina for my treatment of her was not spoken.

Presently Daubeney came in, greeting me quietly though gladly, and asking of my adventures in getting the boat. But the way in which he asked this gave me a foolish annoyance, speaking, as he did, as if no other possible outcome but success had been thought of by him; so that I said as little as I might of the dangers in which I had been. As I told him, at the same time satisfying my appetite with the good food, Fraülein Skoda came in, and with but a glance at me, sat before the fire, having waited, as I believed, for Daubeney to join me before she would come. Having finished my meal, I rose, and speaking of the need to get things ready for our leaving the Castle, went out, thinking in my bitterness that Daubeney and Wilhelmina would be best pleased at being left alone. As I stood up, the pain in my side caught me so suddenly that I had almost cried out, my hand going to my ribs to ease it, and though Daubeney noticed nothing, I saw that Fraülein Skoda regarded me anxiously and wistfully, and though I hurried away, I had time to see that she had been weeping; weeping, as I knew, at my cruel unkindness to her; and how well I remember the last time that I had seen her weep, bitterly, beseechingly—for my own life!

But I went out, stubbornly; for I felt that, despite the soreness of my body and my mind, there was much to be done, and by me. For I would not let Daubeney do more than I could help, or, what I could not do myself; and he, as ever, left all to me, only waiting for my commands to him.

First I went to the gate, where Karl was watching, and more from habit than the expectation of seeing anything, I looked through the grille; and coming openly up the causeway, already within a hundred paces of the gate, I saw one of Count Czvargas' soldiers, bearing a white flag. Bidding Karl stand at the grille, and chiding him for his want of care in letting the man get so near

without being aware of his coming, I told him
to cry out to the messenger, when within easy
earshot, to stand, while I took my place beside
him, wondering what this might mean.   At
Karl's word to him to stand, the man stopped,
and in a loud voice cried :—

"His Excellency Count Czvargas, to him
who is in command of those who have taken
unlawful possession of the Castle Czvargas.
Terms of surrender!   That the person of
the maiden .Fraülein Wilhelmina Skoda be
delivered to him, Count Czvargas.   In return
for which His Excellency will allow all others
who so desire to leave the Castle safely.   I
have spoken!"   And the man grinned foolishly
at his rough manner of delivering the message.

"Tell him," I cried to Karl, "that rather
than submit to such treacherous terms, we
would all gladly starve, and Fraülein Skoda
with us!"   When he heard my answer
from Karl, the soldier bowed gravely and
replied :—

"His Excellency Count Czvargas will
repeat his most gracious offer in seven days"
(by which I knew that he expected the
cannon to reach him by then), "and then,

woe be to all who are within the walls of the Castle Czvargas!" And he turned and walked jauntily away. While I rejoiced greatly at this news, and had cried out in my delight, but for this horrible stitch in my side catching me and making me groan instead. I now went about my further work more gladly than before, knowing that, with good fortune we should likely get a full week's start before the Castle was attacked, and our flight known.

Going to Count Czvargas' room (not caring to disturb Daubeney and Fraülein Skoda even with my good news), I searched carefully to find any papers that might be useful to us; for a long time in vain, until in a drawer, apart from the others, I found a small packet, still tied up, which had been taken, as I saw, from Herr Skoda. These, and as much gold and silver as I found I took, telling myself that I was not robbing Count Czvargas, but taking payment merely for the forced imprisonment of my brother and myself. With these safely bestowed, I left Count Czvargas' room for, I hoped, the last time.

Next I consulted Frau Gretchen with regard to such provision as would be needful

for three days, for that I did not wish to be
burdened with more than we could easily
carry, nor to have to buy food until we were
well away from the region of the Castle and
Count Czvargas' friends. This last I knew
would be the greatest of our dangers, since
his complices were to be found even in
Venice itself, Fraülein Skoda having seen and
recognised among the soldiers of the Count
one of the very guides that her father had
procured before leaving that city; which no
doubt accounted for the easy falling of Herr
Skoda's party into Count Czvargas' hands.
But we were bound for Munich, since, though
farther distant (and indeed partly for that
reason in that if Count Czvargas looked for
us it would more likely be in the direction of
the nearer place), this was Fraülein Skoda's
home, and we knew something of the road
thither.

Frau Gretchen was much cheered by the
near prospect of getting away from the Castle
and the hope of returning again at some time
to her own home, so that I found in her a
very willing help to my plans, leaving to her
care all that was needful with regard to

provision, telling her only to advise with
Fraülein Skoda in any doubt or difficulty. I
told her also to be most careful with the fire,
making it so that at our going away it would
burn slowly and with smoke for as long a time
as possible, for the better deceiving of our
enemies. To this same end I obtained
candles from her, which, before we left, I
placed burning in the guard-room, from
whence a window looked upon the lake
towards the causeway, that while they gave a
light (which could be only for one night, but
so much gained), it would appear that we
were still within the Castle. Of warm clothing
I told Frau Gretchen to take enough, but as
little as might be, that we might be less
encumbered. For ourselves and the men,
we would only take such clothes as we were
wearing (mine being collected from such as I
could find that fitted me most nearly). For
Daubeney, Karl and myself I found two good
pistols each and a long sword; Kaspar and
Johann I did not let have any weapons,
fearing them, at least Johann, who was still
sullen, doing all that he was told to do indeed,
but with a bad grace; but Kaspar was more

friendly, and even cheerful with us at the prospect of getting away.

So we ate our last meal, a great one, in a strained silence of excitement; of hope that we might get quite free, and of fear at our past finding of the length and strength of Count Czvargas' arms. I ate quickly, wishing to relieve Karl, and when I had finished, went out to take my last turn at keeping the Castle gate.

CHAPTER XV.

WE LOSE KASPAR AND JOHANN.

As I stood looking through the grille, I wondered, for the hundredth time, if Count Czvargas would think that we could leave his Castle by any other way than by the causeway. All our chance hung on that! The need for a boat at the Castle was so small, so Karl had told me, that it was used but seldom, and never by the Count. And yet, had Count Czvargas sent Fritz to look for it, or to learn news of the three men who had gone after Daubeney? In either case, I thought, he would hardly have sent one man by himself. So I argued with myself, trying to believe that our chance of escape was greater than, in truth, it was. And this I write here only that you may know how much of anxious thought I had at this time, when all looked to me to get them from the prison to which by my own acts I had brought myself and them.

So, when the sun had gone down and it was quite dark, we repaired silently to the opening from the courtyard to the lake.

First I bade Daubeney go down by the rope, for though my side gave me much pain, yet did I not wish to forego the pleasure of being the last to leave the Castle. The good rope strained under my brother's huge weight, but held him well. Then I sent down the bundle of clothing and the food, directing Daubeney to bestow them carefully under the seats of the boat. Next I made a loop in the end of the rope, and placing Fraülein Skoda so that she sat within this, I, with Karl's help, lowered her slowly and carefully, bidding her keep her face towards the rock and to ward off the sharpness of any projections with her hands: it was hard work, but she reached the boat safely without any hurt, Daubeney receiving her. Then Frau Gretchen was let down by Karl in the same way, without a murmur from her, and then Johann (who showed some hesitation and pretence of fear) went down, and Karl, and Kaspar ; and last of all I followed, slipping down slowly, so that the going down gave me less pain than I had had in climbing up the night before.

All the while that this was doing we had kept a strange, fearful silence ; and no doubt we should have made an odd spectacle, if there had been any to see us—which we all devoutly hoped there could not be.

I ordered Karl and Kaspar to the oars, Johann sitting in the bow, and I in the very back part of the boat, guiding the rudder ; while Fraülein Skoda, Frau Gretchen and Daubeney sat as comfortably as they could in the stern seat. The night was dark, black clouds driving up from the south with a keen biting wind. The boat was overladen, as I had known it would be, so that I feared if a squall came we should be in some danger of getting swamped. As I gave the order to begin rowing, we began slowly to move away from the rock, with a great sense of relief and of dread ; and in a few minutes we had left the Castle behind us in the darkness. The two men rowed silently and well. Indeed we were all silent, listening eagerly for any sound, and casting anxious glances over our shoulders. The camp fires of the Count's guard burned brightly in the distance, the light from them being the last sign that we had of our enemies.

We reached the southern end of the lake without accident, and almost without a word from any one of us. As we neared the road-way, I told the men to cease from rowing, the current, which I knew so well, taking us past the point. Here Johann, as I thought, moved uneasily and raised himself to look along the road, but the sight of Daubeney's pistol kept him from trying to get ashore (as but for this fear he easily might), though I believe he wished to do so. So we passed this most dangerous place in safety, and into the stream, and down it quickly for two miles, each boat's length gained making our minds more hopeful, though our bodies were cold enough in the damp night air. Then suddenly, so that we were jerked from our seats, and Frau Gretchen screamed, the boat ran full against some obstacle in the stream, and water came rushing in at a great rate—where there was no room for it. I guided the boat quickly to the bank, the stream being very narrow, and telling Karl to keep a watchful eye on Johann, we landed, taking our things with us, in time to prevent us from getting wet, save for our feet, though the bundle of clothing and the food were soaked with water. The boat filled quickly through a great ragged hole in the side of it, and in a few minutes sank. So that now we had perforce to get on as best we might by land. We put as good a face upon it as we could, dividing the wet loads between the five of us men, Daubeney, as I suggested, helping Fraülein Skoda, and I coming last with Frau Gretchen. Karl led the way, as knowing most, though little, of the direction we should take. Johann indeed offered to guide us, but whether he knew anything of the way or not I did not wish to learn, only that I would not trust him.

The path by which we went, which indeed was no path at all, having to be made by us through the thick bushes, was rough and uneven, but I was most thankful that the ground under our feet was good and firm, for that I never wished again to have to wade through a bog ; and, even so, I found it hard enough to keep with the rest and to help

Frau Gretchen, for the shooting pain in my side cut through me with each jolt on an uneven bit of ground, making me cough. Soon after we had started to walk a cold rain fell, wetting us to the skin, who before were quite miserable enough. But none complained, not even the good Gretchen, though the walking, to her unused to it, was most toilsome and distressing. But after some time, she sat her down upon a log, and bursting into a wail of tears, said she could walk no more. But Fraülein Skoda coming to her, comforted her, speaking to her and even caressing her as though she were of her own blood, and persuaded her to try to come a little farther. Then I called Karl and bade him support Frau Gretchen, for that I myself could not, so that the way might be made less wearisome for her.

After we had toiled on in silence through the cold wet darkness for another long mile, we came upon a small deserted hut; nor was Frau Gretchen alone in welcoming the sight of it for shelter and for rest. Finding a half broken-down shed near by, we ourselves took what little shelter we could find there, giving the hut to the two women. We got some sleep, but to me at least it was not much comfort, so that the sign of coming dawn was very welcome. Seeing a bright light in the hut, I went there, and found Frau Gretchen busy preparing a meal for us, while Fraülein Skoda came in at the moment bearing an armful of firewood that she had gathered. The others joining us, we crowded round the cheerful fire, our clothing sending out a great damp steam, and we had more pleasure in the simple meal that the good woman prepared from the sodden food than might have been thought, though we had to take it standing or sitting on the mud floor. Moreover, Fraülein Skoda did much to enliven us by her ready flow of talk and laughter, the moody Johann even being cheered by her gay manner; as for me, I envied Daubeney his place beside her, though he took this favour which the gods sent him with an easy carelessness that angered me.

When, having eaten, we began to make ready for another start, Fraülein Skoda came to me, shyly enough, and said that Frau

Gretchen wished to go no farther with us. Now I had had it in my mind to let her go back to her own home, as I believed she wished, as soon as ever this would be safe for us and for herself, seeing that she was a hindrance to our haste ; and yet I wished her to be with us if only for the sake of Fraülein Skoda. But now that she herself said that she wished to remain behind, and Fraülein Skoda was willing that she should, I let her, making her promise only that she would stay in this hut for a full week after we had gone on, so that if Count Czvargas learnt of her going back to her house, we should then be beyond the chance of capture by him. To this end I gave the woman food enough to last her for a week. So we left her, weeping dismally, as we proceeded on our way, Karl lingering behind for a few minutes after the rest of us had come from the hut, to comfort her, as he said.

That we might obtain a fresh supply of food, since that our store was much diminished by that we gave the woman, it became most needful that we should reach some place, where this could be bought, before the next day. But of this I was not fearful, as by questioning Johann and threatening him, I learnt that we should likely get to a village this same evening. Which, after a long weary tramp we did—weary more from the anxiety of our minds and our fears for Fraülein Skoda than from the length of the journey, though she trudged on the toilsome way without murmur of complaint, keeping ever a cheerful look of hope upon her face. Not wishing to attract the notice of the villagers, we stopped at a small cottage, the first we came upon, and asked for food and shelter of an aged crone who sat before the fire. Nor would she have granted it to us, for that my manner was something rough and her coarse dialect most strange, but that Fraülein Skoda came in timidly and helped me. Even so it was plain that the woman was in fear, and yielded only for the sake of the gold piece with which I tempted her. Aided by Fraülein Skoda's help and our willing hands the crone got ready some sort of a supper for us, to which we added from our own small store, and having eaten this, we were all most pleased to take some rest,

Fraülein Skoda going with the old woman to an inner chamber, while we slept upon the floor. For safety, Daubeney and Karl and I took turns to watch; but nothing came to disturb us in the night.

In the early morning I sent Karl out with money to buy food, and also, if he could find one, a good horse. In the space of an hour he returned bringing a great strong animal with him and a large sack of provisions across its back. Not waiting to take breakfast, the woman being much relieved at our going, we once more started upon our journey, keeping away from the village as far as we were able. We travelled now in more comfort, for the horse, besides carrying Fraülein Skoda, bore the bundle of her extra clothing and our food also; so that, unencumbered, and with the anxiety with regard to the maiden taken from our minds, we proceeded on our way in good heart. So much so that I think we spoke too openly of our intentions and of the way that we thought to take, for which I was most sorry later. Our hopes now growing stronger with each mile that separated us from Count Czvargas, we reached, late at night, another village. Here we readily found shelter and a good resting place.

So we went from day to day, until a week had passed since our leaving Castle Czvargas, and no sign of pursuit, and we began to feel gay in our assurance of safety. By this, the pain had almost left my side, so that I only felt a twinge of it when I moved suddenly, or coughed.

But on the seventh night, which we were spending in the cottage of a kindly peasant, and with more comfort than we had known since the beginning of our journeying, an accident befel us that was like to have been our undoing, and which indeed led on to all the troubles and dangers through which we afterwards passed. We had travelled in a roundabout road, asking our way cautiously at each village as we passed it, and were now going in a northerly direction, hoping in the space of another three or four days, with good fortune and fine weather, to reach Gralzburg. The two men Kaspar and Johann, who wished still to keep with us, and whom we now watched with less care or fear of treachery from them, slept in a shed next to the stall where the horse was, Daubeney taking the first watch, and Karl and I sleeping on the kitchen floor.   At midnight I relieved my brother, and at the hour of three I woke Karl for his turn.

To keep himself awake Karl paced to and fro outside the cottage; but the night being bitter, and a cold rain falling (the first that had fallen since the night of our escape from the Castle), he went for shelter and for warmth into the shed where Kaspar and Johann were sleeping.   Here, lulled by the gentle pattering of the rain, standing with his arms upon the rough boards which divided the stable from the men's resting-place, and his head upon his arms, he dozed; for how long, he could not tell, only that he remembered a great blow falling suddenly upon his head, and then darkness.

Daubeney and I waking at the coming of dawn, and wondering that Karl had not wakened us as was his custom, rose and went towards the stable.   Here we found Karl lying senseless, breathing heavily, and by him Kaspar, dead, with Karl's own knife through his heart. But no sign of Johann or the horse. My first act was to stoop quickly and examine Karl's pockets, finding them, as I had feared, quite empty; for he carried all, or nearly all the money that we had, since, from the first, he had always bought such things as we, from time to time, required. Coming to his senses soon after this, he smiled stupidly at us, but for a long time could tell us nothing; but as soon as he was able to speak he told us how it had happened to him. We could not blame him much, for we ourselves had been something careless in our watch of late; yet I was angry, for that he had once before been neglectful of his duty when he had let Count Czvargas' messenger approach so near the Castle gate without seeing him or giving the alarm. But there was no help for it. That Johann had killed Kaspar and thought to kill Karl was certain, and that we were robbed by him of our horse and of our money was all the comfort we had. It was no use to think of trying to follow him, for even if we were able to borrow a horse, he knew the road better than any of us, and would get quicker on the way.   But where had he gone?   Where, we feared, but back to Castle Czvargas?   Yet we could only hope, that dreading the Count's anger more than his pleasure at hearing news of us, he might go otherwhere.   For he would reach the Castle with haste, in two, or at the most, three days, and so enable Count Czvargas to cut off our journey to Gralzburg, if he so wished.   There was little to be gained, however, by such vain questionings; and first we had the painful work of burying the body of poor Kaspar, who had after all served us well, though under compulsion.   By this Karl was able to stand up, though falteringly, and after a little to walk (and during the day he mended fast, more quickly, I thought, than Daubeney or I would have with so huge a lump upon our heads); so we dug a shallow grave by the roadside and placed Kaspar in it, sorrowfully, knowing that he had done nothing to bring about his death on our behalf.   But Karl took his knife, with which Johann had killed Kaspar, and cleaning it carefully, put it back in its sheath—to be used by him at another time.

Fraülein Skoda received the evil news with

sorrow for Kaspar's death, but with a brave show of indifference at what might follow to her and to us from it, and with a trust in my power to get us safely home that was most comforting. We ate our breakfast hastily, and I was glad that, as our appearance did not betoken wealth, our clothing being soiled and torn, I had paid our host the night before for this (so that, being paid, he might provide for us more willingly).

With as much heart as we could feign we started, with only enough money to take us for another day. And after that? Well, after that we must make the most we could of hope!

CHAPTER XVI.

HOW MONEY (MUCH NEEDED) MAY BE EARNED; AND OF A GREAT ALARM.

ALL through that day, as we trudged on, I racked my brains to find some way of helping us, but found none. This, more than the walking, which was easy now, along good roads, wearied me almost beyond endurance. Fraülein Skoda was tired too, though she strove bravely to keep us from the knowledge of it, and, to please her, we even feigned not to notice it. But Daubeney saw it as well as I, and in his simple, earnest care for her, I read the love which had conquered mine. Yet I, too, took the deepest pride in her bravery, but tried to stay my feelings lest they should get beyond my weak control.

So, mostly in silence, we trudged on, Karl leading the way a few paces in front, stolid and determined, giving us more courage by his steady front than he knew or would have believed. We spent most of our scanty store of money to buy bread (for that Fraülein Skoda discovered a few small coins in her pocket), a coarse black bread, which, with water, was our only food ; but Fraülein Skoda ate it cheerfully and with a show of enjoyment, so that we might not think she wished for better fare. We spent the night, sleeping under the stars (saving the little money we had left for bread) ; and I wondered fondly if the maiden would remember that other night which she and I, unknowing, had spent under the same sheltering tree.

So, during the next day we tramped on, feeling hungry before there was a chance of a meal to satisfy the craving. As before, Karl marched in front, silent as ever, speaking only when we first spoke to him, now and then glancing back to see how we were following. After him Daubeney and I, with Fraülein Skoda between us ; he striding along with his giant's body, looking straight in front of him, seeing not what was before his eyes, but our meadows of Somerset, and hedged lanes and the dear thatched roofs— perhaps dreaming of a time when he should

show all these to the maiden by his side;
smiling when I spoke of our difficulties, as if
there were no doubt that I should overcome
them.   Yet there was!   And when the next
morning came, and still no way out of our
trouble, my brother still showed the same
careless confidence in me.   And Fraülein
Skoda too, when, as the day wore on, I told
her something of my fears, smiled bravely in
my face, and said :—

"There have been worse dangers, Master
Frank, that you have helped us from.   So
will you now!"—which had been more pleasant hearing from her if I had had more hope
myself.   So as we went on slowly, painfully,
during that weary, hungry day, I thought of
every way of trying to get food, of begging,
with promise to pay when we were able, even
of taking it with no promise; but with no
good resulting.

By this, we were, as I judged, not very far
from Spätz, near which we did not wish to
go for fear of Count Czvargas' complices, of
whom we knew that there were some in this
town; but rather to go on by a longer way
to Gralzburg, if indeed we should ever reach

so far. So, eating the very last of our food, with empty pockets, tired bodies and grumbling stomachs we lay down again to sleep under the cold stars.

The next morning we were wakened (for we lay not far from the roadway) by the noise of people passing, though the dawn had not yet come. Calling Karl, I directed him to go and ask them where they went so early, and to learn if he could the object of their journey. For, to tell truth, burdened as I was by the constant fear of being followed by Count Czvargas, I thought that these peasants even might be fleeing from him. Presently Karl returned to tell me that the peasants went towards Berlau, a small village near, where that day the people kept holiday. So we followed them, scarce knowing why, but hoping earnestly that some way might be found for us of getting food. Our stiff and aching limbs kept us from travelling so fast as the peasants, but we pressed on, others bound for the same village passing us and laughing at our soiled and broken clothes. When we came to the village, we found it to be quickly filling with people from all parts, and all intent on pleasure, so that we, who wished above all else for breakfast, were, we thought, the only wretched creatures there, the only ones with old and faded clothing.

As we entered the street of the village (if indeed it could be called a street, that was but a narrow road between small cottages), we passed an inn, and Fraülein Skoda, looking timidly at me, touching my arm, spoke :—

"Master Frank," she said, "might not I get some employment here? 'tis likely that there will be much extra work to-day"; and she blushed softly, smiling. While I turned hot and red at the thought of her, timid and gentle, working for such coarse peasants. Yet she clung to the chance, and would not let me go past the inn, till she had tried her plan. Daubeney said nothing, who as I thought should have, so not wishing to be churlish, nor to take upon myself the ordering of her behaviour, with a bad grace I let her go and ask the woman of the inn. In a few minutes she returned gleefully to say that the woman welcomed her most gladly, being over-come with work and the illness of her daughter, and promising Fraülein Skoda food for herself and us if she would help her in the house during the day, little knowing, as I smiled to think, what three hungry men waited outside. Indeed, when she saw us (for, rather than spoil Fraülein Skoda's pleasure in doing something for the common good, feeling also that the house would in some measure afford shelter and protection for her, and some rest, I made no further protest) she cried, staring open-mouthed at Daubeney's giant frame and hungry looks, and holding up her hands :—

"To feed such men as these and you! for one day's work; ah no, it is too much!" But Fraülein Skoda besought her, and at my offering that one or all of us should also help, she yielded, saying that one of us men would be enough. Yet did she not grudge us food when we went in, but seemed to pity us for our sorry looks when all else who came in were happy and well clothed.

The food put a new heart in us, and Karl asking that he might serve, the woman also saying she would have him rather than either of us, Daubeney and I went out. At first we were content to sit outside the inn and watch the passers by; but presently, the sounds of merriment attracting me, I said to Daubeney that we might go towards the market place and see in what manner these Bavarian peasants spent a holiday. So, looking in at the kitchen, where we saw Fraülein Skoda helping at the work most pleasantly, as though enjoying it, and bidding Karl, who was kept busy too, have an eye on the maiden, my brother and I strolled quietly down the street.

As before, Daubeney's great size caused much notice to be taken of us, but of so good-humoured a sort that we thought no harm would come of it, the more so as we only smiled and laughed back the coarse jests which were made at our appearance. But presently we came upon a sight which interested me much more than anything that we had seen for a long while, and which, on me at least, had a strange effect of home-sickness.

In the centre of a ring, made by a number of strong peasant youths, stood one, who in a loud voice, using the rough dialect of the country, challenged any to a bout at wrestling. At the sound of this, so unexpected where we thought there was no knowledge of the sport, I was for going forward and trying a throw with the man. But Daubeney, ever more careful and slower than I, held me back, saying that it would be better to watch one bout before ourselves engaging.

" Let us see first what this man can do before we try," he said. " Moreover," he went on, " you cannot wrestle, remember your wounded side."

" My side!" I cried, astonished, since this was the first Daubeney had said of it, and, as I thought, it was now well, " what do you know of my side?"

" Nothing," he answered, " but what Fraülein Skoda told me," and he blushed, " that you hurt your side when going for the boat." And I made no answer, reddening in my turn at thought of her silent notice of my pain, and of her fear to speak to me about it ; but that she should not fear to talk to Daubeney brought again a jealous bitterness to my heart.

But now my thoughts were turned to the

ring before us; for at the other's challenge a youth stepped out, and casting a small coin beside one that he who challenged had first thrown, faced the man, and in a moment they began. And I saw at once the wisdom of Daubeney's caution, since this kind of wrestling was so different from ours of Somerset, that one of us would have had little chance without some previous knowledge of the playing of it. Scarcely could it be called playing, indeed, for the violence and fury of it, where two small coins (and the honour of being victor) were the only reward. The men used not at all their feet for tripping— this, as we learnt being not allowed, nor clasping of the hands, only that a man might hold his own wrist. Of one thing I was glad, that they wore no boots; for in some parts of our County the brutal habit of kicking with great boots takes from the play all pleasure and comfort. The undercatch was fought for desperately; and this as well pleased me, in that it resembled more than in any other way our Somerset style of wrestling. But these men were not content with a fair throw, but must needs grovel and scramble on the ground, struggling furiously until one made the shoulders of the other touch the earth together. To say when this was done, which was most difficult, was left to the eyes and tongues of those who watched and shouted their outlandish cries of praise or blame, rushing forward and declaring one the conqueror, to the great confusion of the sport, themselves engaging in fierce wrestlings with those who agreed not with them. Yet, for the most part was there no unfairness, and only an excited pleasure in the game, so that he who was declared the winner, was so fairly, and received the praise of all.

In the first match (for as with us there were three bouts), he who had challenged threw the other quickly and fell heavily upon him. But after a short rest of heavy breathing, the beaten man threw two coins down beside the two which the other had left lying and entered the ring again. This time he was declared the winner, and he who had challenged first put four coins down beside the other four, and they met once more. And who won, we learnt, would take the eight pieces of money and be declared the champion until, challenging in turn, he were perchance beaten. But he who had challenged first won, the most of the tussle being fought furiously upon the ground after the men had fallen together. The conqueror, rising, took up all the pieces but one, and put them proudly in his pouch.

For some minutes no one came forward in answer to this further challenge (which the one coin left upon the ground implied); then Daubeney, amid the jeers of the peasants, in his soiled clothing, stepped into the ring, and having, to my surprise and his, found two small coins at the bottom of his pocket, threw one of these beside the other's.

Had it been Somerset wrestling there could have been no doubt of the result, for Daubeney was larger and cleaner built than the peasant. But, in his forgetfulness of this strange style of play he lost the first bout, throwing the other indeed, but not thinking of the need to make both shoulders touch the ground, he went to rise, when the man darted suddenly at him unprepared and turned him quickly upon his back. Daubeney smiled softly only, at being beaten, so that the peasants yelled with pleasure. But when my brother, looking towards the victor, held his one remaining coin in the palm of his hand, regarding it ruefully, a great cry of laughter rose, and many offered Daubeney the money that he needed. Taking a coin from one of these, with a pleased smile, he cast it with his by the others and faced the man again, throwing him easily and taking care this time to drive the man's shoulders to the ground. In the third bout also, Daubeney won, though not so quickly, the peasant playing with much fury. Then Daubeney, picking up the coins, for that he saw a stranger's victory was not so pleasing to the crowd as his defeat, and pressing two upon the man who had lent one, went quickly away with me.

My brother looked at the coins lying in his hand with a whimsical seriousness that was very odd to see. But they were money, not much indeed, but still something of what, at this time, we needed more than aught else.

Then, after another hearty meal, at which, to our displeasure and her own great amuse-ment, Fraülein Skoda waited on us like a serving wench, we lay down in a quiet spot and rested.

What might have happened to us and to Fraülein Skoda, had Daubeney and I been content to stay there quietly until the evening, I cannot say. But we were not, at least I was not; for the sounds of merriment from the village drew me back to look again upon the faces of the happy peasants and their boisterous games, feeling it so great a relief to view their pleasure after the time of anxiety through which we had lately passed. Nor was Daubeney loath to go, seeing that I wished to. We looked in at the inn to see Fraülein Skoda contentedly slaving at the woman's bidding, but, as we gladly perceived, keeping away from the rough attention of the men who from time to time came in to eat and drink. Karl we saw also helping in the kitchen work, obeying orders like a trained soldier.

Thinking it better that we should not be seen together, Daubeney went towards the wrestling ring (where I had rather been), while I walked idly round the place, watching the rude sport in which the peasant youths and maidens were engaged. So, now and then catching a sight of each other in the crowd (I seeing Daubeney more easily than he me), but keeping ever apart, we spent the afternoon, until the sun began to sink in the western sky, while the noise of the revellers became more wild, as they made the most of their one day of pleasure in the year of toil. I was unmolested, save for some jeering laughter at my dirt-stained clothing, for my smaller size kept me from the notice of the people. But, as I saw whenever I came upon my brother, his stature was a constant source of wonder and of remark, and the pretty peasant girls darted many an admiring glance (as well they might) at his huge, handsome form as he slowly and gently pushed his way through the throng, towering over all.

I was just thinking that it was time for us to go back to the inn, when I became aware of a great noise of shouting laughter at the wrestling-ring; pushing my way thither with some difficulty, by reason of the eagerness of the crowd to learn the cause of this, I saw my brother, laughing and protesting, as a number of peasant youths, to the noisy delight of every one who watched, dragged him into the ring. Had I been able to get nearer, even so that I could have cried to him, which from the babel of noises was impossible, we might have afterwards been saved much trouble. But, try as I might, I could not, so that I had to stand on tip-toe and look, hoping that less evil might come of this than I feared would.

For I saw that a powerful man, dressed carelessly in the garb of a soldier (of whom I had seen none until now in the village) was standing in the ring stripped for a wrestle, taunting the peasants for their fear of him. More than this, I knew the man instantly as one of Count Czvargas' soldiers, though that Daubeney did not was plain to see. He had been drinking, and his speech was thick, but, despite that, he was an awkward man to meet in a kind of wrestling which he doubtless understood; still, I had no fear of the result; but, I thought, as my troubled mind urged me, if one of Count Czvargas' soldiers were here, there might be many, even Count Czvargas himself, unless,

as might indeed be the case, this man were
a deserter from the Count's service. ˙

I did not wait to see more, for as soon as I
perceived that by trying to prevent Daubeney
from engaging with the man I should only
make more trouble, and be recognised by the
soldier (who by some strange chance did not
know my brother)—as soon as I saw that
this was useless, I drove my way back through
the crowd, and ran with all my speed towards
the inn. Even as I went rushing blindly
through the gathering dusk, I met three
others, soldiers of Count Czvargas, reeling
along, holding one another by the arm, singing
drunken songs. With my fears increased, I
ran on, caring little whether they saw me or
not, and arrived, breathless and excited, at
the inn. And Fraülein Skoda was not there!
nor Karl anywhere to be seen; only the
woman sitting without concern at a table,
drinking wine. But I quickly changed the
look in her face, when I strode to her, and
roughly shaking her by the shoulder, asked
where the maiden was. Ah! dear God, how
much I suffered in those moments! If time
should count by pain I had been an old man

before I left the inn. At first I could get nothing from the woman but cries of fear, but in a little she told me, whimpering, that shortly after our going away, horsemen, to the number of about eight, had ridden up to the house, and dismounting in the yard, had come into the kitchen.

"And," she said, "when your maiden saw them, she just threw up her arms, and dropped down in a dead swoon. And he who seemed to be an officer among them, a huge, black man, came to her, and without so much as a word to me, lifted her in his arms, and went outside. There, though I tried to stay him, for which my only answer was an oath, he mounted his horse, and galloped back upon the road to Spätz."

"Alone?" I cried, "alone?" squeezing the woman's arm so that she cried out; but she answered me. "Yes," she said, "the maiden only with him; the men he called to follow him, as soon as they had had enough to eat and drink."

"But Karl," I cried, "our man Karl, what of him?" But at that she only shook her head stupidly, knowing nothing of him, while

I cursed my foolhardiness in entrusting Wilhelmina's safety to the man.

Though this talk had not taken long, yet had it occupied more time than I had wished, for the woman was slow of speech and in great fear of me ; but I bethought me now of the soldiers' horses, and hurrying out to the stables, I found no less than six strong chargers munching at their food. Hastily choosing one of these, that looked the fleetest and least tired (where all were travel-stained and jaded), I mounted him and rode out into the road.

CHAPTER XVII.

OF OUR LAST MEETING WITH COUNT CZVARGAS.

WHEN I came into the road, I dismounted, and fixing the horse for a moment, ran in to tell the woman what to say to Daubeney when he returned, and to ask the way. But I could not find her, and as I hurried out I again met my brother coming in, who at sight of me, held up 'twixt his thumb and finger a golden ducat, smiling with boyish glee. But I ran to him, and shaking him violently by the arm, astonishing him beyond measure, cried hotly :—

"You fool! while you were playing with Count Czvargas' soldier, the Count himself has come and carried away Wilhelmina!" and as he stared oddly at me, giving him no time to speak, I went on. "Get a horse, man —in there," I pointed to the stables, "and we will follow him and get her back; quick, quick!" I cried, as, without a word, he turned and went off quietly towards the stables. But he could hurry too when he had a mind, and surely now, I thought, if ever, he would feel the need.

In a short space he joined me, and together, without further speech between us, we urged our horses through the darkness, along the unknown road to Spätz.

The road at first was good, and our horses carried themselves (and us) most nobly, though they had been tired before we started, as, for several miles, we went on steadily without a word between us. But our minds were active enough! Mine was filled with bitterness and anger at my own carelessness, and my unjust words to Daubeney, since, but for my desire to see the holiday-makers at their play, he and I would have been at the inn, or near it when Count Czvargas came there, and so none of this had happened. And Daubeney, knowing my quick temper, had let me put the blame on him, knowing, as of old, that when my senses became clearer, I should see how wrongly I had judged him.

When we had ridden thus for more than an hour, our horses showing signs of the pace at which we had driven them, we went more slowly, our minds burning with impatience at the need for care of them. Yet with no plan formed, only the hot desire to come upon the Count, and force from him his unwilling captive. Presently it came to me that we must be on another road than that to Spätz, for, reaching the top of a steep hill, we saw, stretching before us, a great open plain for many miles without sign of any town or village such as we were looking for. N r was there any cottage where we might inquire the way. When I told my fears to Daubeney, breaking the silence between us for the first time since we had left the inn, he answered that he thought we should have been nearing Spätz by this.

So we turned and walked our horses slowly back upon the way that we had come, for that they were not fit to go faster, Daubeney's indeed stumbling badly under him as we descended the hillside. After going thus for about a mile, we saw, some distance from the road, a small light burning. Going ,-wards this, and finding it to come from a cottage, we tried to learn some news of the best way to Spätz from an old man, who of all the household had alone remained at home, the others being still at the merry-making. But whether we mistook his meaning, or he ours I know not, only that, following his direction, we wandered blindly through the whole night, until, just at the first sign of coming dawn, we came by chance upon the outskirts of a village. By this our horses were in a parlous state, for the roads and la.. es by which they had brought us were bad and difficult; and we ourselves were stiff and weary with our hopeless search. But, coming to the village, our spirits rose most wonderfully, so that we urged our horses on for the last time, and they, jaded and lame, scenting the stables, and seeming to know their way to them, broke into a painful ambling trot.

Yet was there little cause for gladness, except for the hope of getting more surely on the road to Spätz where we made certain the Count had gone. But on foot, for that our horses could not take us further.

Suddenly my brother broke the silence in a cautious whisper. "Stay!" he said, "I know this place; it must be Breczin, where I bought the horse which I soon after lost. Come, let us visit the rascally innkeeper who dwells here, and see if aught can be learned from him. See," he added, as our horses, without guidance from us, turned into a side lane, " these know the way too!"

So, in a short time, we came to the inn, standing apart from the rest of the village. Entering the yard of this, silently, and getting from our horses, which were glad enough to stand and rest themselves, we went to the house, and after some delay were able to enter by a side door, and from this to make our way into a large kitchen where was a fireplace with a dying woodfire in it. Though the light was beginning to come outside, yet in here, with the shutters to the windows, we could see nothing for the darkness, but stood listening for any sound, and indeed marvelling that our coming in, for all that we had been most quiet, had not been heard.

First to our ears came the easy sound of a tired sleeper's breathing, and turning our eyes towards the place from which this came we saw a dark mass which slowly showed itself to be a man's figure. Stealing on tiptoe to a window behind the sleeper, carefully and without noise I drew the shutter a little open; for a moment the faint light of the dawn fell upon the man, but only for a moment, for with one hand to my mouth to stay the cry which nearly came from it in my surprise, the other closing the shutter quickly, I saw Count Czvargas!

He was lying on a couch drawn to the fire, dressed to his boots, his hat fallen to the floor; at his left hand upon a table within easy reach of him a great pistol, and his right upon the scabbard of his sword which lay beside him. He stirred uneasily at the thin ray of light that I let in, but his tired breathing did not change. Daubeney and I, for some moments stood staring at the man and at each other, too astonished at our good fortune to think what to do with it. Fraülein Skoda, too, I thought, must be here, in this same house. Well, it would be strange indeed if my brother and I could not secure her once again from the Count Czvargas. But we dare not leave him to go look for her, nor would it be of much avail with our spent horses to try to get away from his pursuit.

All this ran through my mind as the man's breath came and went once, then, pointing to the pistol, I made a sign to Daubeney to take it. This he did quickly, without sound, and held it pointed at the Count's face within three feet of him. While I, treading softly, went near, and bending over him, caught his sword, and began to draw it slowly from the sheath. But he moved, wakened by our presence or the dawn (for that the shutter which I closed but did not fix had swung a little open, throwing a faint light into the room), and I had but time to snatch the sword and step back to Daubeney's side before Count Czvargas was upon his feet glaring at us, and fumbling stupidly for his weapons.

Then, to my wonder, Daubeney spoke, my brother! who had always in the time before left this to me. Yet was I glad in that he had a clearer knowledge of what should be done and of our danger, whilst wild hopes and thoughts of Wilhelmina rushed through my mind, and no plain words to speak.

"If you make a sound," he cried in a low voice of threatening, the pistol within a pace of the Count's head, " I will shoot you like the dog you are! Turn and go out by that door!" and he pointed to the door by which we had entered.

For some moments, stupid from his heavy sleep, Count Czvargas stared from one to the other of us, his hateful mouth open, and his blinking black eyes dwelling upon me; then he made as if he would step towards us, his hand again going to the empty scabbard, while I wondered more and more at the change in my brother's manner, as he cried, still pointing to the door :—

"Go! I will count three : one, two ——";
but the Count did not wait, but, turning on his heel, went out, we two following close upon his steps. When we came to the yard, which was now well lighted by the dawn, though the sun was not yet up, Daubeney gave me the pistol, bidding me keep it pointed at Count Czvargas.

"Now, Sir Count!" he said, stepping near to him and holding out his hands, "I am minded to give you a show of English Wrestling or of Sword-play, and I will let you choose. Which shall it be?" and my brother even smiled with pleasure at the curious part that he was acting, while I marvelled silently. Count Czvargas' mouth worked in his fearful rage, as his eyes went quickly round the yard and back to Daubeney, the veins upon his forehead standing out black, and, but for my pistol, would have flung himself upon my brother.

"Come! which?" said Daubeney again, still smiling sweetly.

"Swords!" he said at length; and Daubeney, stepping back to me, took the Count's sword which I still held, and, measuring it with his own, and finding the two to be of equal length, handed the Count his, an ugly grin of malice and of satisfaction passing over his evil face as he eagerly clutched it, and thinking to take my brother unprepared, made a great cut at him. But Daubeney guarded easily and with such carelessness as he might have shown had he been playing with me and the swords of wood. How often have he and I gone over this great fight, standing against each other, sword in hand, and playing at the scene!

As, in his fury and hatred, Count Czvargas

dashed at my brother, he kept him off, still with a faint smile playing about his boyish mouth which I think angered the Count the more, while his eyes flashing, the hot breath hissing between his clenched teeth, a foam coming from his mouth and marking his black beard, he tried to get past Daubeney's guard. But he, I thought, strove rather to humble the Count Czvargas than to injure him, contenting himself with keeping off the other's angry blows ; till, seeing a chance, he made a great cut at the Count who parried clumsily to the right, the back of his hand down and the sword-point up, and Daubeney's sword coming against his with great force, struck it from his grasp, so that it fell clattering on the stones, and slid along to my feet. Then into Count Czvargas' eyes there came a great look of fear and the dread of coming death, as he stood defenceless before my brother from whom he could look for no mercy. But Daubeney quietly stooped, and picking up the Count's sword put it with his own on the ground beside me, and standing up, faced the Count again, regarding him silently. They made a fine pair, the two giants, facing each other; though in my eyes at least the advantage lay with Daubeney with his clean fair face and honest eyes.

While the two had been fighting, and more now, I saw that Count Czvargas was listening eagerly, thinking no doubt that the host of the inn or other friend of his should come, attracted by the noise; but none came yet, and I was impatient at the delay and wished that Daubeney had made an end of our enemy, as he easily might, instead of playing with him thus. For now he spoke again:—

"You only play with swords," he said, "like a half-taught boy. Now I would wish to see if you can wrestle, as you said you could. But not with my brother, who is too strong for you, and can beat me; but with me. Come, let us make a bargain! If you throw me, you shall go free! not as you once let me, treacherously, but free in truth to go where you will. If I throw you," and Daubeney stopped for a moment (out of breath, I thought, with the longest speech of his life) and shrugged his shoulders, "my brother here and I will take the maiden Fraülein Skoda from your care and ——"; but before Daubeney could say more (and methought he had said quite enough), the other attacked him with so great a sudden violence that he was like to have been thrown ; yet was he not, though it was the fiercest attack that I had ever seen. The two were well-matched, for though my brother's strength and nimbleness were something greater, yet was the Count fighting for his life. Soon Daubeney, with a great double heave to one side and the other, using my own pet breast stroke, threw him on his side. But he rose again at once, and dashing at Daubeney with fresh fury clutched him with the undercatch, and, lifting him up, sought to "break his back," as he had seen Daubeney do to me, by dashing him to his feet and throwing all his huge weight upon my brother. But he, so that I warmed with pleasure at the sight of him using my trick again, feigned to fall, and turning his body quickly, with a great swing cast the other heavily on the ground, his head striking a sharp stone, and a thin stream of dark blood trickling from him as he lay still.

And Daubeney, leaning over him, smiled quietly, while I ran to him and cried :—

"Go you and find Fraülein Skoda! quick, man! Enough of this play! Find her and get her ready for our going away. Some of his soldiers must come soon—they are here now!" I cried, "I hear them, go you quick and see who it may be." For we heard the sound of galloping which stopped at the inn.

As he hastened away, I found myself wishing that he had run his sword through Count Czvargas at the first, knowing, as we did, that he had a friend in the host of the inn, and likely enough many others in the village. Now he lay senseless on the ground, and we must bind him securely, if we could, and get away with all speed.

The noise of fighting at the front growing loud, and seeing that Count Czvargas lay so still, I ran through the house to see if my brother might need any help from me. In the lane before the house I saw Daubeney crossing swords with the frightened keeper of the inn, and, by his side, Karl, whom we had lost, and whose honesty to us we had begun to doubt, fighting desperately with the faithless Johann—faithless to us at least, though faithful to his master the Count Czvargas. When I saw that I should not be needed, having no fear of the result of this fight, I hurried back to try to find Fraülein Skoda, looking first into the yard to see the Count still lying where Daubeney had thrown him.

I soon found her; for, disturbed by the noise of fighting, she had come to the door of her chamber and was looking fearfully out. There I met her. At sight of me she cried out with joy, throwing her two hands into mine with so glad a look upon her face that I found no words to say, only regarding her with love and wonder.

"You have come again!" she said, almost sobbing, "to save me—you! and yet I knew you would!" and she blushed prettily at her words; while my eyes were blinded by a great mist of joy at this her trust in me; and yet by what little chance it had come about that I was here at all, she could not know. Moreover, I had done little or nothing; to Daubeney belonged the praise which I was hearing from her lips. But I said nothing, only drinking in her beauty. Then, suddenly, scarce knowing what I did, holding her hands still in mine, I stooped and kissed her forehead. But even as I did this I saw a look of fear leap into her eyes, while her body stiffened and her face went white at sight of something that she saw behind me. And in a moment, as I turned quickly to see what it might be, I felt the sharp burning pain of a knife entering my shoulder, which, but for the warning in Wilhelmina's eyes, had pierced my heart, and then great arms were thrown under mine and the Count's hands clasped behind my neck in a most deadly grip as, struggling helplessly, he forced me down and down. I was power-less to grip him, and felt that I must be crushed by his huge strength, when, with a cry of fear and anger, Wilhelmina came to my aid, striking, how feebly God only knows, but yet to much purpose at the Count's face. He, starting back, surprised at this attack from her, whom I can but think he in his own way loved, loosened his hold, so that I was able to twist round and face him, gripping him close. And with a strange delight I held him, and drove him, giant thought he was, back through the doorway to the yard again and threw him with my leg behind his heel, easily.

But he was up and at me again, nor was I sorry for it, since it was a great joy to me to have my arms round a man's waist again ; but he caught me fiercely with the undercatch, and as he did so I felt my half-healed rib snap with a terrible pain ; but I let myself fall, and as his hold of me loosened, I jerked my arms under his, and caught him as he had held me. His hands then went to my throat, and as he clutched it, striving to force me away from him, for all the pain of my side I gripped him with all my arms' strength, pressing harder and ever harder till I felt one of his ribs and then another crack under them, and as each went the hold of his fingers upon my throat winced, yet stayed there. At that I left his body, and grasped his wrists, trying to free my throat, but in vain ; then I caught his body again, desperately, above the hips, and with all my strength, bending my knees to get a better spring, with a groan of pain at the greatness of the effort, I lifted him, still clinging to my throat, and flung him over my shoulder to the ground. But only at the last moment did his hands leave their hold, so that I too fell back with the force of my own throwing, and before I could recover myself he was at my throat again, drawing me back upon himself; but I was able to wriggle from his grasp and to get heavily upon my feet—the long weary night, the loss of blood from my shoulder and the pain of my side telling upon me too soon—not quickly enough to prevent Count Czvargas from doing the same, as, his teeth and gums showing like a dog's snarl, his black eyes gleaming with hate and revenge, clutching at my throat again, with a sudden hurling of his weight forward, he threw me backwards with himself upon me, his deadly grip still holding me, his black face close to mine, blood trickling from his mouth, while I felt my eyes starting from my head and my face swell with the horrible sense of being drowned, and I gave myself up for dead, killed, after all, by this man. But, just as my senses were leaving me, and my sight, I heard, as in the far distance, a shout in a familiar voice; then there was a great rush, and the glitter of a knife, and the Count's hold of me loosened, while some one dragged him off from me. And I gave a great sigh, taking in a huge breath of God's good air when I had thought that I had had my very last of it.

In a moment or two I was on my feet again, and though my side gave me much pain, and my throat (so that for some time after I spoke only in a hoarse whisper), yet was I able to rejoice at being alive still, and to watch with interest what was passing before me.

In the doorway stood Wilhelmina, looking towards me with frightened eyes, with yet a show of deep relief in them, and wonder. At my feet the Count, dying or dead, blood flowing fast from the wound of Karl's vengeful knife; over him Karl leaning with so deep a flush of hatred on his face, and in his eyes the gleam of gratified revenge, that I was startled by it, for that his face was changed from its sullen stupid look to that, as it appeared to me, of some other man. A pace behind him, Daubeney, watching and listening too; and behind him the terrified keeper of the inn, his arms bound, and the sleeve of his shirt stained with blood from a sword

wound.   All listening to Karl, as with the
pent up fury of three years let loose, he
taunted and spurned the fallen man.

"You devil, murderer, hound!" he cried,
"destroyer of peaceful homes, liar and thief;
now have I avenged the murder of my father,
my mother, and my brothers, and with the
same knife that you used upon them, though
I have waited long for this day! and of my
sister ——"; but at the mention of her his
face went black with hate and his mouth
worked as if he could not speak the words
to tell his loathing; then he stooped lower
so that he looked into the Count's dying eyes,
and cried aloud as though he feared his
victim might not hear:—

"Go now to Hell, where you were be-
gotten, and burn for ever for your devilish
crimes!" and he spat in the man's face, so
that we shuddered at the sight, while a shiver
ran through the Count's body, and with a
choking sigh, death came to him.   At that
Karl stood up, and plucking the knife from
where it had given the death wound to Count
Czvargas, he flung it far away from him, and
looked round at us as though aware for the

first time of our presence, and without another word resumed his ordinary look and mien, standing silent and indifferent as of old, with only a flushed cheek and glistening eye to show the passion which he had felt.

CHAPTER XVIII.

HOW AT LENGTH WE REACHED MUNICH, AND OF THE DAYS THAT FOLLOWED.

But I walked up to Karl, and grasping him by the hand, said (nor was the huskiness of my voice altogether caused by the soreness of my throat) :—

"If, Karl, we get through our troubles, and arrive safely home, whatever you wish and I can do, count as done, for, man, you saved my life!"

"As you did mine," he answered, grinning with pleasure.

"I yours?" I said, astonished; "when?"

"When you delivered us, Herr Frank, from the Castle Czvargas!"

"Or when I led you in?" I said, smiling, but he only shrugged his shoulders.

Then I turned to where Fraülein Skoda had been standing, but she was gone; to her room, I hoped, to get ready for her further journey. I asked Karl, then, how it was that Count Czvargas had been able to take away the maiden without his knowledge. At which he told me how he had spent the night.

Karl had been sent by the woman to get something from a storeroom at the back of the house, and while there he heard the sound of horsemen approaching, and presently a number of his old comrades rode into the yard, and putting their horses in the stables, went into the inn. Karl followed them in quietly, to make sure of Fraülein Skoda's safety from the sight of these men, and looking into the kitchen, was pleased to see that at their coming, she, as he thought, had retired to her chamber. For the Count having entered the house from the front of it, he had seen nothing of him.

Believing, as he did, that the maiden was safe, he thought it best to hide himself from these men and to keep a watch upon them. To that end he followed after them when they left the inn, hoping that he might see Daubeney or me and so tell us of the presence of these men in the village. By some mischance he did not get a sight of either of us, but after an hour, leaving the soldiers all drunk with wine, he returned to our inn to learn from the woman that Fraülein Skoda had been taken off by Count Czvargas and that Daubeney and I had followed after them. Taking one of the horses, he hurried after us, arriving at Breczin about an hour after the Count. Wondering at not finding us here (for he had learnt from the drunken talk of the soldiers that they were to follow the Count back by way of Breczin, of which news we were ignorant, so that Karl was able to get in the track of Count Czvargas when we did not), he was able, by watching carefully for a chance, to get a sight of Fraülein Skoda; but only for a moment, though the sight of him cheered her most wonderfully. Then Karl returned on foot to our village, his horse being weary, and hearing no news of us there, once more made for Breczin, taking another of the horses for his journey. As he neared Breczin again, going warily, he was overtaken by the man Johann, who, recognising him, galloped on to give warning to his master. But Karl was able to keep up with him, and so soon as they reached the inn and had dismounted, attacked him with his sword. The innkeeper coming to Johann's aid, Karl was hard beset when Daubeney arrived; he, engaging with the keeper of the inn, enabled Karl to successfully attack Johann, whom he killed. Daubeney was content to wound the innkeeper in the arm and to bind the frightened wretch. As this was being done, Fraülein Skoda came running out to tell them that Count Czvargas was killing me; at which Daubeney and Karl had rushed through the house into the yard, and Karl had given the death stroke to the Count at the moment that I had thought my end was come.

Nor in all this time had my mind been without the thought of Wilhelmina; of my kiss, of her start of fear at sight of the Count behind me, and of her timely help to me when in his deadly grip; even when I was, as I thought, about to die, the thought of her was with me. But now, when my eyes strayed round the yard, looking for her, they could not find her. So, for that the need to get away from this place urged me, bidding Daubeney find and bring Fraülein Skoda, and Karl the horses, I went through the house, and mounted my horse with pain and difficulty, but with as little show of it as I was able, and giving the word, we all started quietly away, without so much as a word to the blubbering innkeeper whom we left to perform the last sad offices to the bodies of his whilom friends. Yet, as we went, I saw a look of expectation in his face, as he glanced uneasily up the road which we were taking.

.The reason of this look I learnt when we had gone near half of the way back to Berlau. For here we came to a lane leading from the road, and were in some doubt whether to follow it or not, but in the end kept to the road, because of the lane's unevenness (though Karl said that it would shorten our journey by a mile or more), for that I found the pain of my side hard enough to bear even upon an even road. As we went on, we saw in the distance, coming towards us, three horsemen, riding furiously. They took the lane where it came from the road and went along it, passing by us without seeing us; but we, keeping under the shelter of some trees till they had gone, saw that they were the soldiers of Count Czvargas, returning in all haste to join their master, having been summoned, as we learnt upon reaching Berlau, by a messenger from the Breczin innkeeper.

Coming to the place where the lane met the road again, we saw where Daubeney and I had left it, not having seen in the darkness and our haste that the road went here in two directions. But now we were not sorry, for all that we had passed through much labour and anxiety during the night, since our purpose was now happily accomplished, where, had we taken the right way to Breczin, no one could say what might have happened to us or to Fraülein Skoda. By such little accidents are the lives of men changed.

As we came near to Berlau, we met four others of Count Czvargas' men, walking; and by a most lucky chance were also able to keep from being seen by them, so that they hastened on their way without knowing who had taken their good horses.

So we went slowly and quietly on. When we came to the village, we were surprised to find the people in a state of excitement, meeting us with looks of fear and trouble.

When to their eager questionings whether we had seen Count Czvargas we answered that he was dead, they were filled with a great joy of deep relief. Nor, when from a heedless remark of Karl's, they learned that it was by his hand that the Count met his death, could they do enough for us, or show Karl sufficient honour; so great had been their dread of this cruel robber. So that we, who had entered the village beggars, glad to wrestle publicly in hope of gaining a few wretched coins, and the most gentle of us to serve in a common inn at the order of a peasant woman, were now treated with such respect as is shown to nobles. And, indeed, feeling unworthy of it, and too tired to accept the rejoicing gratitude of the people in the way that they wished, were like to have given offence by pleading great fatigue, but for Karl who went off in the midst of a noisy throng, leaving us to get what rest we might. The woman of the same inn received us gladly as honoured guests (driving a thriving trade so long as we were there), and Daubeney and I went to the bedchamber that she showed us, and remained there until the following morning.

While we were resting at the inn (for that my rib might have the better chance of healing, and my shoulder also which was stiff and sore, we stayed there for three days, enjoying much the quiet and peace after all our time of trouble) many came from all parts to see us, and especially Karl, who had brought about the death of their enemy Count Czvargas. And indeed Karl was like to have got harm from the constant rejoicing of which he was made to be a partaker, this taking the shape of much drinking of wine, so that on two nights our faithful follower returned late to the inn with most unsteady steps, helped on each side by friends less steady than himself. We were, therefore, not sorry to bid Good-bye to these good people and to start, as we earnestly hoped for the last time, on our journey to Munich. On our promise that Karl should return as soon as might be and repay her (for that on his way back to his own country he would need to pass through Berlau), the good woman supplied us willingly with enough money to take us to Gralzburg, where we knew that we should be able to obtain a loan from our uncle's friend.

During this time Wilhelmina, afraid no doubt of the noisy crowd of peasants, kept much to her own room, coming out to us only when a meal was to be taken (and as we could see employing her time with needle and thread upon her worn clothing), and then sitting silently and talking little to Daubeney or me except in the answering of questions. But my lips still burned with their touch of her forehead, longing that they might so touch it again—with no Count Czvargas near to spoil all.

So, followed by the loud blessings of these poor villagers, we mounted our horses—ours since we had possessed ourselves of them to the equal loss of Count Czvargas' men—and slowly travelled by way of Gralzburg to Munich.

During that quiet happy ride (for the pain in my side quickly went, leaving me as well as ever again, save that I would feel where the rib had been broken if I jarred it, or a cold wind blew, or rain) my eyes were opened to the foolishness of my thought that Daubeney loved Wilhelmina ; for, watching him more closely than before, I saw that though

he treated her (as who would not?) with
kindness and the utmost courtesy, yet did not
his look brighten at her presence nor his face
flush when she spoke to him, as was the case
with me. Nor indeed have I ceased to
wonder yet that he did not love her. But
that I loved her, as I knew long before, so
I knew now, and better. But she? That
could I only learn from herself, and by asking
her. Which, in truth, is a harder work than
any man knows who has not himself been in
like case. Nor need he look for help from
the maiden whom he loves, for that she will
be so innocent and coy, seeming to know
nothing of what is in the young man's mind
to tell, that he must needs do all the talking,
as best and bravely as he may.

But I had no wish to speak, at this time, to
Wilhelmina of my love for her. For as we
came nearer to Munich she became more sad
at the thought of getting back to the home
where she could not look for her father,
weeping silently as she rode, so that my
heart ached for her, though no words of comfort came to me to speak. So, with my great
love for her growing with each step of the

way, and my desire to help and comfort her in her distress almost more than I could bear and not cry out, we arrived at length, safely and most gladly at Munich.

We repaired at once to the house of our uncle, and to our loud summons to him he came, standing in the doorway and screwing up his eyes at us with his head thrown forward and his hand going constantly through his long beard. So that at sight of him, part with pleasure and part from amusement at the odd sight he made, I laughed aloud. And he said :—

"Yes, that indeed is my nephew Frank, and no other. But, God in Heaven! where have you been this great while? and—and whom have we here?" this last he cried loud in a voice of joy that was most pleasant to hear, as he ran towards Fraülein Skoda. "Mina, Wilhelmina," he went on, "by all that is most strange and happy! Ah me, but this will be a glad day for your father!"

"My father!" she cried, with a great catch of tears in her voice, as we all regarded my uncle with astonishment. "Is he—is he well? Where? Oh, take me to him!"

"Where is he?" said my uncle, smiling widely, "here, child, here in my house! and to-morrow about to set out for a certain Castle of Czvargas to seek a wandering maiden named Wilhelmina!" and at this huge joke my uncle clapped his thigh and laughed most unrestrainedly (as I had heard him laugh once before). But Fraülein Skoda slipped from her horse, and taking his hand, urged him to bring her to her father, which he did at once ; returning presently to give Daubeney and me fresh welcome, Karl leading the horses (glad as we to have reached their journey's end) to the stables. Our uncle then showed us to the bedchamber that my brother and I had each slept in when here before, and we put on again the clothes that we had left, which had not been touched since. And in our clean neat coats and breeches we scarce knew each other.

Herr Skoda greeted us most joyously, thanking us again and again for our care of his daughter, and regarding me, as I thought, keenly as he did so. During the evening he told us how, when his party was attacked by Count Czvargas, he himself had been wounded and left on the ground for dead ; but recovering from his swoon, had wandered through the forest seeking Wilhelmina, but, as we knew, without success. Thinking that she would be a prisoner of Count Czvargas, he had returned with all the haste he could, which was not great, to Munich, and immediately upon arriving there had fallen into a fever, so that his wild, wandering talk was not understood by his friends. As soon as his senses returned to him, he dispatched a messenger to the Count offering a ransom for his daughter's freedom, if indeed she were a prisoner to him, but getting no reply to this (though that Count Czvargas had received it we found when the packet of Herr Skoda's papers was looked into), he determined to go himself with the strongest force that all his money and influence could procure, and try to get back his daughter ; our happy arrival with her coming about the day before that on which he had intended to depart.

If our fresh clothing made so great a change in the looks of Daubeney and me, what shall I say of Fraülein Skoda, when on the following day, she and her father having returned to their own house, Daubeney and I went thither to visit them? For though in all the time of trouble through which we had passed together her attire was arranged with a maiden's care for such things, yet even her desire to appear tidy to us could not take away from her dress the stains of travel and of sleeping out of doors, nor had she been able to give that attention to her beautiful hair in which a maiden so delights. Now we saw her as we had known her at the first, though to me at least it seemed new, striking me afresh with an abiding sense of wonder and admiration. Yet all the care which she had bestowed upon her hair could not keep it from breaking in crisp waves over her forehead, and the long quaint plaits so carefully tied each with a dainty bow served only to render more noticeable its shimmering beauty, so that I longed to draw its gold to me and bury my face in the glory of it. Yet the more I longed to do so, the more fearful did I become to try, and as the days passed and only a few more remained before we must start on our journey home (for that our uncle was preparing to send a shipload of merchandise to England, and us in the same ship), my desire to speak to Wilhelmina became greater as my courage grew less. I chid myself for my cowardice, and each night determined to speak my mind before the next time that I lay down to sleep; and each night still found me with the words unsaid.

Nor did she herself give me any encouragement or hope beyond that which I had found before, regarding me kindly indeed, but shyly, as if afraid of me. As the time for our going away drew nearer, she became more silent, and when I might be alone with her, which happened but seldom, she would seem to busy herself with her embroidery, stitching quietly while I looked and loved, hardly daring to break the pleasant silence with any foolish words of mine.

CHAPTER XIX.

THE END—OR THE BEGINNING?

But on the last day of all—(for to-morrow, at noon, Daubeney and I and Karl would start for Venice in the company of our uncle's train of merchandise)—when, having made some excuse to my brother, I repaired alone to Herr Skoda's house, I found Wilhelmina sitting idly with her embroidery in her lap, looking out of the window; and when at my coming she turned her face towards me I saw that her blue eyes, which I loved so well, were filled with a soft mist of tears; and, before I knew what I was doing, I was at her side, kneeling and holding both her white hands in mine, covering them with long-held kisses, and pouring out my love in hot words that I would not remember if I could. And a smile came into her eyes and a quick pink colour to her cheeks, as, with a choke in her voice that went to my heart with a great throb of

T

glad pain, she stooped her head to mine and placed a soft kiss upon my forehead.

Ah me! that such joy should come to a man, and to me! It fills me still with the wonder of it. And she whispered back my words to me, calling me her King and Hero, so that I had to stay her with my lips to hers. King! Hero! I, who in all that time struck but one blow at our enemies, and that with the handle of a clumsy oar at Karl and missed; once indeed I fired a pistol blindly in my rage and wounded the Count Czvargas; and once again I held a pistol pointed for some weary hours at a craven's head, whom I had well nigh murdered as he knelt defenceless before me. So that her words of praise, in that I deserved them so little, brought a flush of shame to my face, as I told her how that, but for her help and Karl's the Count Czvargas had been like to have killed me (so that she shuddered at my words); and how that Daubeney my brother had slain men with his own hands. But she struck my hand lightly with her own, and laughed a bright peal of merry laughter, so that I laughed too, not knowing why I did.

" Master Daubeney!" she said. "Yes, he is indeed brave and strong and has slain men! but I love best him who commands— the King who plans and labours with his more wakeful mind; though," she added with a sly gleam of pride and fun, "my King is strong too and can wrestle and swim." So that I put my arms about her and held her to me till she cried :—

"You will break my ribs too, like that!" After a little I said, bantering her: "Yet it seemed to me that you liked my brother well enough in those first days when we were together in the Castle Czvargas?"

"Yes," she said, smiling, "I liked him well enough, and thinking to please you, who I knew loved him, I showed my liking openly."

"Yet you showed no open liking for his brother," I cried.

"No," she answered, with her face upon my shoulder, so that I scarce caught her words, "because, because I liked him much too well!"

I stayed long that day, until the evening stole upon us together and the hush of twilight, finding us divinely happy and content.

As I was about to go I asked Wilhelmina a question: "Are you glad or sorry, Mina," I said, "that your father did not find you in the forest?" And she looked up at me, her eyes twinkling, and answered me :—

"Are you glad or sorry, Frank, that Master Daubeney was taken a prisoner by Count Czvargas?" And my tongue found no words to reply. . . .

When the morrow came with its bitter parting, our love, new, complete, wonderful, kept us from feeling all the grief which our separation would bring. For Herr Skoda, though he approved of his daughter's marriage to me, who, as he said, had saved her life and more than her life, would not, as I fondly wished, let me take Wilhelmina back with me to England.

"No, Master Frank," he said, "go you home and tell your father and your mother, and in two years' time, when my little Mina is older, you may come and take her from me, if she still wishes to go"; whereat he looked oddly at her, so that she blushed prettily, and her eyelids fluttered in the way that I had learnt to love so well; "remember that I have her only; when she is gone, I shall be alone; let me have her but a little longer now that you have brought her safely back to her old father!"

So, with many hearty handshakes and waving of kerchiefs, Daubeney, Karl and I rode out from Munich. In due time we reached Venice, where Signor Vanzetti welcomed us with exclamations of surprise and pleasure; and so to ship, Karl returning alone to Munich where he had promise of employment from my uncle. But here, as we afterwards learned, he did not stay long, being taken with a strong desire to see again his own home country. Thither, therefore, he went, and as at first seemed strange to us, met Frau Gretchen, safely housed again in her old cottage, and in a short time married her; so that he and she now live within a few miles of the place where they and we passed some days of trouble and danger, and where Karl for three weary years had waited for his revenge. I hope and doubt not that the two are content, for though the wife is something older than the husband, yet is that, as I think, no reason why their lives together should not be peaceful and happy.

As for Daubeney and me, we embarked, and after a slow and rough passage arrived safely and gladly at Plymouth. And oh! the sight of the English coast, the cliffs, the green fields, and the sweet landscent, such a delight as it was to us! Without delay, we procured good horses, and hastened on our way to the dear old home, arriving at length at Wivelis-combe at about the hour of noon, one year, to the very day, since Daubeney's going away. On our way thither we had talked over many plans for coming to the house, quietly, so as not to startle our mother, or by sending a quick messenger before us to tell of our coming. Yet in the end we did nothing, but just rode up the drive to the house steps.

Bess, grown taller and more womanly, was the first to see us. At the sight of us she gave a great cry of surprised delight, and throwing up her arms, ran wildly into the house crying for her mother; so that all chance of a quiet breaking of our news was lost.

Soon our mother came out to us, waiting in the great hall, she saying no word, but with tears of joy running down her cheeks, she kissed and embraced us together and by turn, while our father, grown so old in those few months that it struck us, his sons, with a keen pang, stood behind and shook each of us by a hand when our mother and Bess could let him have one of them.

As we became quieter, we looked at our mother more closely, and found her the same dear little lady, but older, so much older! thin lines of silver in her gold hair, and marks of pain and anxious waiting in her pale, thin face. She could not leave her hold of us, but must go with us to the dining hall, and keeping a hand of each, sit between us as we ate our food (as well as we might with a single hand) under the caresses of Bess and the gloating eyes of our father. Nor, in the rejoicings at our own safety, was our faithful Bellew forgotten, so that the account of his death was the first that we told them as they sat over us. And at this day, the stone to his memory, placed there by our father, may be seen in the Church.

The questions! So thick and fast that we could not answer them. Indeed, for weeks, questions were asked and many still unanswered. But in the evening, as we sat in a happy group, and Daubeney and I, but mostly I, told of our adventures, I saw that my mother regarded me long and very wistfully, while I, finding myself seeing in her blue eyes those others which had followed me sadly as I went from Munich, blushed, and my mother smiled and sighed, and turning to Daubeney, her hand upon his, said :—

"You, my son, have changed nothing since you went away—the same quiet, dreaming, giant boy! but Frank," and she looked at me again more keenly and lovingly, "you went away a boy and have come back a man!" And I blushed again, while Bess clapped her hands, not knowing, as I did, that our mother had learned, as women will, how I had changed in those few months, and that some other than she now claimed my best love. So, shyly, I told them a little of Wilhelmina and our love for each other, leaving Daubeney to say more about her than I cared to ; and this he did so simply and pleasantly, that I found myself hot with his praise of her and with my pleasure at his kind words.

So, by slow degrees, we dropped again into the old way of life, the steady English way, though to me it was not quite the same. As for studies, though Daubeney returned to them most readily, I would have none of them. Even the pleasures of wrestling and of sword-play had something less of delight for me—in all things was there that one presence wanting that I had learnt to desire so greatly.

But in this time we were pleased indeed to see some of the colour and the fulness return to our dear mother's face, and the look of deep care and suffering pass away from it. Thus it came about, to while away the weary time that must pass before I see Wilhelmina again, I have thought to put down some of those passages which happened to Daubeney and me, thinking it might take three or perhaps four weeks in the writing. But, what with my want of aptitude for the phrases, and the interruptions of boy's games of wrestling, and my mother's coming in to see if (as I quite believe) Daubeney and I

were really back again and not a dream (and
coming in, would but stroke our hair or put
her cheek to that of one of us and go away
again without a word), and what with my
father's questions of the language, habits and
manners of the people in those countries
through which we had passed (in all of which
I constantly referred him back to Daubeney
for fuller news than I could give), and what
with Bess, who every day and more keeps
running in to ask if I have come yet to the
kissing ; what, I say, with all these interruptions and difficulties, my simple story has
taken me many months ; yet I put down my
pen with a fond regret, in that it has been a
great pleasure to me in the telling.

So, in less than a year's time, as we have
settled it (for twice have I received and sent
letters to Wilhelmina), I shall once more
journey alone to Plymouth, to Venice and to
Munich ; and to the Castle Czvargas ? who
knows ! but after Munich I shall not be alone,
she, my Love, will be with me, and she and
I will journey the rest of our way together.

THE END.

9 783744 735483